ZOE BARTON

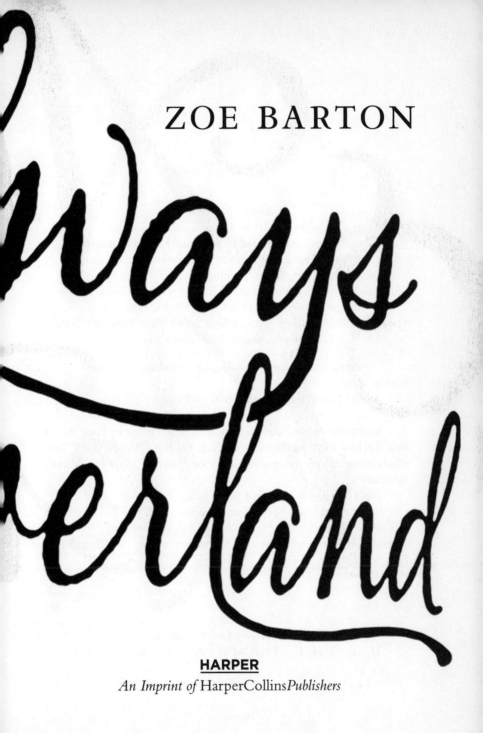

HARPER
An Imprint of HarperCollinsPublishers

Library of Congress Cataloging-in-Publication Data
Barton, Zoe.
    Always Neverland / Zoe Barton. — 1st ed.
        p.   cm.
    Summary: Ashley is whisked away from her home by Peter Pan to
help the Lost Boys with spring cleaning, but this "Wendy Girl's" love
of adventure brings changes that are not enjoyed by all of Neverland's
inhabitants.
    ISBN 978-0-06-196325-4 (trade bdg.)
    [1. Adventure and adventurers—Fiction.   2. Peter Pan (Fictitious
character)—Fiction.   3. Never-Never Land (Imaginary place)—
Fiction.   4. Fairies—Fiction.   5. Sex role—Fiction.   6. Christmas—
Fiction.]   I. Title.
PZ7.B28562Ash   2011   2010045623
[Fic]—dc22   CIP
                                                              AC

Typography by Erin Fitzsimmons
11 12 13 14 15   LP/RRDB   10 9 8 7 6 5 4 3 2 1
❖
First Edition

To Morin,
who would have made
a great Wendy girl

CONTENTS

Tree Shopping Is Canceled

I didn't recognize Tinker Bell when I first saw her.

It wasn't completely my fault. It's not like I got a very good look.

At the time, I stood at the tippy top of a stepladder, trying to reach the second highest shelf in the upstairs hallway closet. That was where we kept the Christmas ornaments and all the lights. Exactly what we needed on the first day of winter vacation.

My motives were perfectly innocent, but when something thunked behind me, I *still* jumped about a foot and a half.

"Whoa," I muttered, steadying myself and turning to look.

A golden light pressed against the window, no bigger than my fist. At first, I thought it was just a car headlight or something, but then it *fluttered* a little.

I rubbed my eyes and looked again, but the light was gone. Suspicious, I started down the ladder.

Unfortunately, I never got the chance to peek outside. Dad walked into the hallway, tugging his tie into place. "What are you up to, Ashley?"

"Nothing," I said. "Getting the ornaments before we go pick out the tree."

Mom's voice came from their bedroom. "Richard, if she's trying to peek at the presents, stop her, will you?"

The word *presents* pushed that golden light out of my thoughts. I whirled back to the closet. On the *very* top shelf, behind Dad's fancy Polaroid camera, I caught a glimpse of silver wrapping paper patterned with green wreaths and realized something very important.

This was where Mom had hidden the presents.

If I just had two more seconds alone, I would've found them myself. And what kid *wouldn't* investigate less than a week before Christmas?

"You heard her," Dad said, tousling my hair. "Hop down."

I clambered down the rest of the steps, thinking fast. I'm an expert at talking my way out of trouble, after all.

Then I cleared my throat and said, loudly enough for Mom to hear in the next room, "The Sixth Amendment in the Bill of Rights clearly states, 'In all criminal prosecutions, the accused shall enjoy the right to a speedy and public trial, by an *impartial* jury—'"

I had been invoking the Bill of Rights in family disputes since a US history unit in third grade. It usually worked.

Folding up the stepladder, Dad laughed, just like he always did.

But Mom was usually harder to convince. She's a lawyer, so she had a lot more practice arguing than my father (he's a botany professor).

In a wry voice, she called, "You'll have to forgive us for being so suspicious, Ashley Gwendolyn Delaney. We *have* caught you searching the house for presents before. Every Christmas since you could walk, actually."

Okay, so maybe history wasn't helping my case, but it *did* bug me that I got in trouble the one time I wasn't really doing anything. "But I *was* just trying to get the ornaments," I protested, crossing my arms over my chest.

"Relax, Ashley—you're not going to be punished," Mom said, which was a huge relief.

Then Mom came out of her room and leaned against the door frame. She wore a velvety green dress with her nice pearls, a sheer golden shawl, and high heels; and she looked even prettier than usual. But it definitely didn't look like the kind of outfit she'd wear to go Christmas tree shopping.

"Why are you so dressed up?" I asked, suddenly worried.

"Holiday parties. First, cocktails with the other professors in your dad's department. In"—Mom checked her watch—"yikes!—fifteen minutes."

"Then your mom's firm has a party a little later," Dad added.

They'd forgotten.

All my plans for picking out the biggest, greenest, fullest, most beautiful Christmas tree in the whole town completely fell to pieces, and my parents didn't even notice.

I didn't give up that easily though. When Mom slipped back inside her room, heading toward the mirror above her dresser, I followed her. "But you said that we were going to get a Christmas tree tonight. You promised."

Pausing to put on an earring, Mom smiled the way she does when she thinks I'm exaggerating. "Really?

When did I do that?—Richard, you might want to hide that ladder, just in case Ashley's tempted to look again while we're gone."

"Good idea." Dad began carrying the stepladder downstairs.

"Last year," I reminded her as she looked into the mirror, concentrating on applying her lipstick. "When we waited to get a tree until Christmas Eve, and there were only two scrawny ones left in the lot. You said that this year, we would get one as soon as school let out for Christmas. That's today."

Mom's face fell. She *did* remember. "Oh, sweetie—"

"You promised *again* when I reminded you at Thanksgiving," I said, a lump in my throat. My whole evening—my whole *Christmas*—was ruined.

"Ashley, I'm so sorry. I completely mixed up the dates."

She meant it, so I tried to be as understanding as I could. "It's okay. As long as we can go first thing tomorrow morning."

"Well," Mom said uncomfortably, "I have to go to work tomorrow."

"On Saturday?" It was hard to believe that she had stuff to do on the *weekend* before Christmas.

Mom nodded. "And Sunday. And Monday too, actually. I would get your dad to take you, but—"

"Finals to grade. Due first thing Tuesday," Dad

called up the stairs. "Sorry, sweetheart."

"Looks like we'll have to go tree shopping on Tuesday afternoon," Mom said.

I couldn't believe this. I waited *all* month for school to let out for Christmas, and when the day finally came, my parents couldn't even spare *one hour* from work to go tree shopping. "But that'll be the day before Christmas Eve," I said. "All the good trees will probably be gone. *Again.*"

"There's really nothing I can do," Mom said apologetically.

It was hard to believe *that,* too. Miserable, I just looked hard at the mirror—the family portrait taped to the glass, the anniversary card Dad gave Mom wedged in the frame, and the wooden whistle hanging from the corner on a piece of twine.

"Please, don't make that face, honey," Mom said, tucking my hair behind my ear. "We just have a really big case coming up, right after the holidays."

I would have tried to argue a little longer, but below us, the doorbell rang.

"Babysitter's here!" Dad said, jogging to the front door.

"Oh no! Where's my clutch?" Mom said, rushing back to her closet and digging through the purses on the shelf.

"Who is it?" I asked.

The front door squealed open, and Dad said, "Hello, Megan!"

Wrinkling my nose, I trudged down the stairs. Megan was one of Dad's students. She was okay, I guess, but she wasn't the most fun babysitter ever. Or the most talkative. She usually paid more attention to the TV than to me.

"Hey, Ashley," Megan said politely. "How are you?"

"Fine," I mumbled. I knew that no one would appreciate me saying that my Christmas was ruined.

"Megan! So glad you're here!" Mom said, clacking down the stairs, a small gold purse in her hand.

"We're running a little late," Dad told Megan with an apologetic grin as he shrugged on his jacket. "As always."

"Ashley, come out to the car with us, please?" Mom said, grabbing her coat and dashing out the door. Dad followed her, and I followed him, shoving my hands deep into the pocket of my hoodie.

"Okay, Ashley," Mom said as I came down the steps. "I have a compromise for you. On Tuesday, how about we all drive up to the mountains and find one of those Christmas tree farms? *They* certainly won't run out of good ones."

"Then we'll make cookies. And eggnog," Dad added.

Mom gave Dad a look, like this wasn't part of the

7

original plan, but he pretended not to notice.

I couldn't help smiling. "Okay."

"In the meantime, here's my iPod," Mom said, pulling it out of her purse and pressing it into my hand. "I uploaded all of my favorite carols, so it should help you stay in the Christmas spirit. But please be careful with it."

She almost never let me borrow it, even though she'd promised that I could have my own as soon as I turned twelve. The metal was cool against my skin. "Thanks, Mom."

"Love you, Ashley." She kissed the top of my head. "Give us a hug fast. We've really got to run."

I hugged Dad good-bye. Then there was this weird noise, like crowing, on the other side of the backyard.

"Did you hear that?" Dad asked me, grinning. We both turned to look. But all we saw was the tree house and the woods behind it darkening in the twilight. "Think the neighbors bought a rooster?"

"Doubt it." Mom stared into the woods too, a tiny smile on her face. "Ashley, maybe you should play outside for a while. Who knows? You might make a new friend."

I snorted softly. She knew as well as I did that I would be the only kid on the street for the *whole* break. Even Michael McKinley—my best friend—had already left town for the holidays.

Then Mom trotted down the driveway and climbed into the car. "Pizza's on its way. Be good for Megan. We'll be back as soon as we can. And just so you know, you *will* be in trouble if you peek at the presents again," she added as Dad sat down beside her and turned the engine on.

Dad blew me a kiss and started to drive off, and Mom waved out the window while the car rolled down the hill.

Suddenly, I really didn't want them to go, and not just because of the tree. Half the fun of decorating for Christmas was having my parents at home and not distracted with work.

I know it was kind of stupid to feel this way, but I almost felt like crying. Being left behind with the babysitter wasn't the best start to my vacation.

Then I thought I heard a worried sort of tinkle, like the ring of a bicycle. I looked up, toward the noise; but as the car turned down the street, I heard a loud, wet pop, like a water balloon bursting, *and*, very distinctly, a boy's voice saying *"Oww!"*

I glanced back. The red taillights of my parents' car disappeared around the bend.

"Hello?" I said, looking around. "Is anyone there?"

No one answered, but near the tree house, the bell sound rang out again, louder and clearer. I looked. That same golden light from earlier zigzagged among the branches and then hovered in space like a hummingbird.

"Hey!" I ran across the yard to investigate, but the light had disappeared.

Hoping to get another glimpse, I climbed up to the tree house. Nothing.

I took a seat, a little hidden behind the railing, and peeked past it, pretending that this was a stakeout. After a few minutes, I put on Mom's headphones to listen to some Christmas carols. I thought the little light might come back out, the way squirrels do if you're very still and they forget you're there.

I waited and waited.

The only lights I saw were the Christmas kind wrapped around the trees across the street. Even our neighbors, the McKinleys, were more ahead on their decorating than we were, and they had left town to go skiing over the break.

I wished they hadn't. I missed Michael. Whenever he came up to the tree house, we pretended it was a castle we had to defend from invaders, or a ship targeted by pirates, or a cabin deep in the wilderness, where bears clawed the garbage and wolves howled at the moon.

Unfortunately, it's not even half as much fun to pretend alone.

With Michael gone, and my parents working all day, it was going to be a *long* weekend waiting for

Christmas to come.

I almost thought that if the whole vacation was going to be like this, then I couldn't wait for school to start again. At least *there* I had people to hang out with.

I shook myself. What was I thinking? Vacation was *always* better than school.

I just had to figure out some fun things to do until Tuesday. I started eyeing some of the evergreen trees in our backyard. If we didn't have a Christmas tree, I could always practice hanging lights and tinsel on a few firs outside.

Better yet, maybe I could cut down a little one and set it up in my bedroom. It couldn't be *too* hard to handle a saw.

I was still trying to figure out the best way to break into Dad's tool closet when the pizza guy drove up.

When I went inside, my hands were pink with cold, and Megan had already dished up a couple of cheesy slices, the grease pooling at the bottom of the plate.

I picked one up and sat down on the sofa, next to Megan.

She didn't say anything. She was too busy watching a boring made-for-TV movie, set during the holidays, where some bank robbers disguised themselves as Santa.

I sullenly picked at my pizza. It was Mom's favorite— half pepperoni and half pineapple with onions. I wondered why she had ordered it that way if she was just going to leave.

If Dad were eating with me, he would've traded my onions for his pepperoni.

Suddenly, I wished that my parents had taken me with them. *That* was how desperate I was.

This was turning out to be the worst vacation ever. Lonely *and* boring.

After another slice of pizza and about half an hour, I left my plate in the sink and headed for the door. But as soon as my hand touched the knob, Megan called, "Where are you going?"

"Outside to play." I wanted to continue my stakeout at the tree house. I figured it would be easier to see the light in the dark.

"It's a little late for that," Megan said sternly, which basically meant *no way.*

Arguing wouldn't help. I knew from experience that she would pretty much let me do whatever I wanted— *unless* it might get her in trouble. If Mom and Dad came home and saw me in the tree house at night, Megan would *definitely* get in trouble.

So, without having anything better to do, I said good night and climbed up the stairs to my room. When I fell asleep, I was still debating about whether I should risk climbing out of the window or just go back to the tree house in the morning. . . .

I woke up suddenly about an hour later.

It only took me seven seconds to realize that there was a strange boy in my room, standing at the foot of my bed.

2
I Learn a New Use for Super Glue

I shouted and threw the first thing I could reach—
my pillow.

It hit the boy in the back of the head, and he tumbled halfway across the room. I jumped up and threw my other pillow as hard as I could.

The boy was quicker than I expected. He darted out of the way, and the pillow plopped to the floor with a small *whoosh*. I was out of pillows, so I glanced around for something else. A library book sat beside the bed. I picked it up and got ready to aim.

But the boy wasn't standing anywhere in the room now.

He was *flying*, hovering in a corner and breathing hard. He held a sword. It was about the length of my arm, and it cast gold reflections into the shadows. His hair sprang out in wild blond curls all around his head. I couldn't tell if his shirt was made out of leaves or if he'd attached leaves to the fabric, but he definitely had a weird outfit on.

I was so surprised that the book slid out of my hand. "Oh!"

"Oh?" the boy repeated mockingly. He scowled. "That wasn't very nice."

With his free hand, he rubbed his head. Something wet glinted on his cheeks.

"Are you *crying*?"

"Of course not."

But he wiped his face with the back of his hand and sniffed suspiciously.

"I'm sorry. I didn't mean to hit you *that* hard." But in the back of my mind, I was pretty impressed with the way I defended myself. It wasn't every day you got to fight off nighttime intruders.

"It wasn't the *pillow*," he said, sheathing his sword. "It's my *shadow*."

"Your shadow?"

"Over there."

The boy pointed across the room. A dark, flat figure was struggling to open the window. It was shaped exactly like the flying boy, right down to the wild curls and leafy clothes, and it was having trouble getting the window up. Shadows must not be very strong.

Something about the scene seemed very familiar—like something I had read in a book or seen in a movie.

With a sudden, electrifying thought, I turned back to the boy. "I know who you are! You're Peter Pan!"

"Of course I'm Pan. Who else would I be?"

Peter Pan and his shadow in *my* bedroom? I pinched myself to make sure I wasn't dreaming. It definitely hurt.

I couldn't believe my luck! My winter vacation just got a *lot* more interesting.

The legendary boy flew to the window. When he grabbed his shadow's shoulder, it slapped his hand away and tried more frantically to lift the window.

"None of that now," Peter ordered. Then he looked at me and added, "My shadow hasn't gotten away from me in a very long time, but it got stuck under the moving metal carriage outside and snapped right off."

It took me a couple of seconds to realize what *exactly* he was talking about. "You mean, my parents' car?"

He didn't answer. Instead he dragged the shadow away from the window. It reached up and tickled Peter's stomach. Peter laughed, and when his grip loosened, the shadow made a break for it.

But Peter was faster. Before his shadow reached the

window, Peter tackled it again. Then boy and shadow wrestled, tumbling across the rug. They banged into my nightstand so hard that my lamp toppled and fell.

I was still a little stunned, but I couldn't just stand there forever, especially when Peter looked like he could use some help. So, I jumped off the bed, picked up the book, and whacked the shadow. The poor shadow stopped fighting Peter and held its injured head in its hands.

I waited for Peter to thank me, but he just sat down, cross-legged, pulling the shadow closer by its foot.

The shadow tried feebly to get away, hooking its elbow around my desk chair. That didn't work. Peter just dragged shadow and chair until his own ankle and his shadow's foot touched.

Then he looked at me expectantly. "Aren't you going to attach it?"

I stared at him. To be completely honest, I had no idea how to get someone's shadow to stick on. That wasn't something they taught in school.

But I did know how to find out.

"Just a sec," I told Peter. I went to my bookcase and searched the shelves. I knew that Grandma Delaney had given me *Peter Pan* for Christmas a couple years back, but it took me a while to find it. "Here we go."

I flipped through the pages, skimming until I came to the part I wanted. "It says here that Wendy *sewed* your shadow on."

"Yeah, sew it back *on*," he said, sounding impatient.

"Sew? I don't know how to sew!" I didn't even know if we owned any thread.

Peter jumped up, still holding his shadow's foot. Tipped upside down, the shadow flailed both flat arms, trying to steady itself.

"Hold on," I said quickly, worried that they might leave before Peter did anything really exciting, like teach me to fly. "I think there's some Super Glue in the kitchen."

I crept out of my room and down the back staircase, walking close to the wall to avoid the creaking floorboards. Peter flew just behind me, holding his shadow in a headlock all the way down the stairs and into the kitchen. With his leafy shirt and the struggling shadow, he looked so out of place flying over the sink that I had to pinch myself again—to make sure it was all real.

Then I opened the junk drawer and started combing through it. I knew the Super Glue was in there somewhere. We heard brakes squeal in the next room.

Peter looked around wildly, one hand on his sword. "What's that noise?"

I pushed past dried-up pens and several pairs of scissors to the back of the drawer. "A car chase. The TV's on." Megan had turned up the volume *really* loud. No wonder she didn't hear me shout earlier.

"TV? Would the Lost Boys like it?" Hovering a couple feet above the floor, Peter pushed open the door to the living room, peeking his head through curiously.

"No!" I grabbed his foot and yanked him back.

Now that he stood on the ground, I could see he was only a little bit taller than I was. He glared, cheeks bulging, like he was about to start shouting.

Legendary or not, I wasn't going to let him get me in trouble. Especially when I was doing *him* a favor.

"Stop it!" I said sharply. "Do you want to get caught?"

That got his attention.

"The great Pan is never caught," Peter said, but he said it very quietly.

"Maybe so. But I'm not taking any chances." I didn't want Mom to find out and reconsider the trip to the Christmas tree farm.

I held up the tiny bottle of Super Glue and gestured toward the stairs.

Two and a half minutes later, we sat on the floor in my room, and Peter forced his shadow to the carpet beside him, pinning its arms to its sides. The shadow hung its head, as if accepting its defeat.

"Mind lifting up your foot?" I asked Peter.

Instead of just raising his leg like I expected him to, the boy flew up and hovered several inches off the ground, feet still extended toward me.

"Thanks." I unscrewed the top of the Super Glue and reached toward Peter's foot.

The boy flew very slightly out of the way. "Are you *sure* this will work?"

I'd figured that I had an 80 percent chance that shadows could be glued. But I told Peter, "I'm *positive*. Wendy would've done it this way, if she had Super Glue. It won't even hurt."

After hearing that, Peter relaxed a little, and he did let me grab hold of his ankle. I squeezed a thin line of Super Glue across the boy's muddy heel, and then I reached for the shadow. It kicked me a couple times, halfheartedly—it didn't hurt; it felt more like a puppy trying to squirm out of my lap—but I managed to squish the shadow's heel against Peter's without getting any Super Glue on my hands. I let it go and dealt with the other foot.

Luckily, the glue held, even when the shadow clutched my bed frame and tried to drag itself away from Pan. I was almost as happy about what I'd done as Peter was.

"Gluing is even better than the sewing. Why didn't I think of this before?" Peter crowed and started doing a few backflips. When he stopped, his shadow swayed a little and put a hand to its head dizzily.

Then Peter zipped toward the window, not looking my way once.

Worried that he really *would* leave, I said quickly, "Since you woke me up and all, would you mind telling me why you came to visit?"

I was pretty sure he would just say that my window was closest when his shadow snapped off, but I was hoping to steer the conversation to other things. Like flying, for instance.

He turned back, grinning, his fists on his hips. "I came to take you back to Neverland, of course."

He made this announcement as if it were the most obvious thing in the world, but I stared at him, almost afraid to believe him.

"Neverland! Really?" I glanced at the cover of *Peter Pan*, filled with illustrations of pirates, fairies, Indians, and even mermaids. I might get to meet a *mermaid*!

And I had wished my parents had taken me with them. Neverland sounded *much* better than any stupid grown-up party.

"You *are* the newest Wendy girl," Peter said.

"Wendy girl?"

Peter looked at me in a shrewd, judging way. "On second thought, I don't know if I *should* take you back to Neverland. You can't be very smart."

"Smart?" I was a little bit offended. I wasn't used to being called dumb. I mean, Mom usually said that I was *too* smart for my own good.

"You just keep repeating everything I say," he added thoughtfully.

I couldn't argue with that. "How am I supposed to know what a Wendy girl is? I only know about Wendy Darling, the one who went to Neverland with her little brothers."

"You do? You know about our adventures?"

I didn't remember them all that well, but I nodded anyway, picking up the book with his name on it and waving it in front of him. "You're famous."

"Of course I am," Peter said with his cockiest smile. "Let me explain." He lay on his back, floating lazily in the middle of the room the same way that other people float in a swimming pool. "Well, Wendy Darling was the first Wendy girl. You're her granddaughter or great-granddaughter or great-great-granddaughter or something like that."

I looked at the book in my hands again in wonder. When Grandma Delaney had given it to me, I'd just thought she was trying to get me to read more, but she must've been a Wendy girl too! She must've been trying to help me get ready for the day I would meet Peter Pan.

Peter yawned. "I've been bringing Wendy girls to Neverland *forever*."

The way he said *forever* reminded me of how my classmates complained about doing their homework, or cleaning their rooms, or whatever boring activity they couldn't wait to finish. Maybe I should have been insulted, but I was too excited.

"I want to make friends with a mermaid!" I said. "And meet Tinker Bell. And Tiger Lily! Oh, *and* cross swords with Hook."

Peter stood up, giving me a sharp, measuring look. "Well, that last one is impossible."

"Oh no," I said, disappointed. "Have you already killed him?"

"No, not yet, but *I'm* the only one who can fight Hook," Peter said. "Everybody knows *that*, Wendy girl."

"My name is Ashley," I said quickly, realizing I hadn't introduced myself.

But Peter continued on like I hadn't spoken. "Besides, you're supposed to come and help the Lost Boys with their spring cleaning."

"Aren't you a bit early?" I asked. "It's still winter."

"Not in Neverland," said Peter.

To be honest, I didn't like the sound of that. I mean, this was my Christmas vacation. I didn't want to spend it doing chores. But making friends with the Lost Boys sounded *great*. Anything was better than sitting here alone, waiting for my parents to take me tree shopping.

"Can we leave *now*?" I asked.

Peter sat up, considering. "I guess so. All we need is Tink." He flew to the window, opened it, and let out a sharp whistle.

A little golden light reemerged from the woods beyond the tree house, the same one I had seen earlier. It headed straight for the window, tinkling like bicycle bells. I stepped forward, eager to meet the fairy. Maybe we'd be friends before I even reached Neverland!

I barely had enough time to duck before the golden light zoomed right where my face had been.

Then she landed on Peter's shoulder, her hands on her hips.

Now that she wasn't moving I could see the figure within the light—a tiny woman, very curvy, with a rose-petal dress and very blond hair. She was glaring at me.

"Hello, Tinker Bell," I said as politely as I could. I wanted to make a good impression. Especially since it seemed like she was already angry with me for something. "I've always wanted to meet you. You're even prettier than I imagined."

She chittered angrily. I frowned, wondering what I had done wrong. I was almost sure that it wasn't anything I said.

"Tink, don't start bugging the Wendy girl again," Peter said wearily, but the light zoomed straight at me a second time.

I ducked behind the bed for safety, but Peter was

faster. He plucked the little fairy out of the air mid-flight. As Tink struggled and squirmed, trying to break his grip, Peter shook her over my head. Golden specks fell from the fairy onto my hair.

"Since I'm famous, I bet you know what this is," Peter said.

"Fairy dust?" I guessed. It felt like warm rain, making me smile. Happiness bubbled up inside me, a lot like soda on an empty stomach, tickling a little. I rose immediately into the air. "Whoa."

Peter grinned. "I was *going* to say that all you need to fly is a happy thought, but you must've already found one. Maybe you do have some potential as a Wendy girl. You learned to fly pretty fast."

"I'm good at flying?" That must've been an even *happier* thought, because I rose higher and started bobbing up near the ceiling.

Tink let out a furious, defeated wail.

"Stop it, Tink!" Peter said, giving her a little shake. "You do this every time you meet a Wendy girl. I don't know what your problem is."

Neither did I, at first, but then I glimpsed the book on the table.

Then I was pretty sure that I knew *exactly* what Tinker Bell was so upset about. It was right there in the same scene I'd just read in *Peter Pan*. Tink had attacked the original Wendy when the girl had given Peter a kiss. Tink was probably jealous of me for the same reason. But she was being silly. I wasn't like Wendy. I wouldn't ask Peter for a thimble or a kiss or anything. If Tink and I were ever going to be friends, she would have to know that.

"Tink, I just want to go to Neverland. I don't even *like* Peter," I said in a rush.

"You don't *like* me?" Peter repeated. He sounded very confused, like it couldn't be possible.

I was so embarrassed that I lost a grip on my happy thought and started to sink. "Well, not like *that.*"

"Like what?" Peter said.

"I don't *like* you like you," I said.

"Like me like me? Now, you're starting to repeat *yourself.*" Obviously, he still didn't understand.

I think Tinker Bell did, though. She snorted, crossing her arms over her chest and shaking her head darkly. I didn't take that as a good sign.

Peter began to pace the room again. It was kind of funny to see him walking across the air above my window seat. "None of the Wendy girls has ever *not* liked me before. Maybe I *shouldn't* take you to Neverland."

A weekend all by myself. No mermaids, fairies, Tiger Lily, or Lost Boys to befriend. That was a terrible thought, and I fell to the carpet with a muffled thud.

Tinker Bell turned to Peter and started chattering

excitedly again. I didn't need a translation to know that Tink was agreeing with Peter.

"But then I heard the whistle. . . . And I did promise the Lost Boys before I left," Peter continued, still pacing. "Kyle was really persistent. He's never had a Wendy girl."

Seeing a glimmer of hope, I latched on to the idea. "And didn't you say that you needed a Wendy girl to help the Lost Boys with the spring cleaning?"

"That's true," Peter said thoughtfully. Tink shot me an angry look.

I tried not to look smug. "I'll just pack some things, and we can go."

Afraid that Peter would change his mind again, I raced around my room. I unzipped the big pocket of my backpack and scooped everything out. My textbooks, my folders, and binders fell to the carpet in a heap.

Peter Pan was the first thing I packed. I figured I might need it. Maybe the book would tell me how the original Wendy won over Tinker Bell.

Then my toothbrush and toothpaste from the bathroom. And after hesitating for a second, Mom's iPod. Mom always said you needed good music to survive long flights.

If I was going to take Mom's iPod, I might as well risk taking Dad's camera, too.

Peter stood by the window, tapping his foot impatiently.

"Two more minutes," I promised.

I crept outside my door and down the hall to the closet. The door creaked when I opened it. I froze, but the only thing I heard downstairs was the TV show Megan was watching.

Unfortunately, I had another problem. The camera was on the highest shelf, and I'd forgotten that Dad had hidden the stepladder. I stretched as much as possible, but I couldn't reach higher than the shelf just below it.

Maybe most kids would've left without it. But I was pretty sure Mom and Dad would *never* believe my story without evidence. I would need pictures to prove I'd really gone to Neverland.

Neverland. The happy thought gave me that fizzy feeling in my stomach again, and I rose up almost three feet in the air.

"Cool," I whispered, grabbing the camera. I didn't even stop to peek at the Christmas presents.

Then I soared back down the hall, kicking to make myself go faster, afraid that Peter might leave without me.

"Sorry!" I flew into the room. Peter was still waiting by the window, arms crossed, with Tink on his shoulder. They both watched me, frowning.

I pushed the camera into my backpack and zipped it up. Landing, I shoved my feet into my sneakers without stopping to tie the laces, and I grabbed my jacket and shrugged it on.

Last, I scribbled a note and left it on my bedside table, where someone would definitely find it.

Mom and Dad,
Off to Neverland. Be back by Christmas.
Love,
Ashley

3
We Play Catch over the Milky Way

*I*t was one thing to start floating around inside my house with a carpet to cushion me if I fell. It was a completely different story to jump out my bedroom window and trust that a little fairy dust would keep me from breaking my leg.

With my backpack on my shoulders, I sat on my windowsill for a minute, working up my courage. Peter gestured for me to get on with it, his eyebrows raised high. (I got the impression that I wasn't the *only* Wendy girl who got stuck on her window ledge.) I couldn't stop staring at the thorny bush that grew right below me and imagining how much it would hurt to land on it.

Peter got tired of waiting. "Happy thoughts," he reminded me with a wicked smile, flying forward like he was going to pull me off.

"No, wait! I'll jump!" *Mermaids*, I told myself firmly, and with a deep breath, I placed both hands on the windowsill and shoved myself off.

I floated. Seeing that I wasn't going to fall made me so happy that I started to rise—past my window, above the roof.

"Wow." Everything looked different from this height. All the trees seemed so much shorter, and in the dark, our driveway looked like just a gray stripe that cut our grassy front lawn in half.

"Let's go then," Peter said, flying ahead. I followed eagerly, scissoring my legs so I could catch up.

"You don't need to kick," Peter said, laughing, as we flew over my driveway. "You're not *swimming*."

My face grew hot, and I stopped kicking. I wobbled slowly through the air while Peter zoomed down the street. Afraid of being left behind, I started kicking again, but I still didn't go fast enough. Peter was already several houses ahead of me before he noticed I wasn't right behind him.

"None of the other Wendy girls were this slow," he said, perching on the top of a street lamp to wait.

"That's why I keep kicking," I explained. "I don't

know any other way to go faster."

"Why are you wobbling around so much?"

"I think it's my backpack," I said, embarrassed. "It keeps throwing me off balance."

Tink zigzagged around Peter's head, chittering impatiently.

Peter translated. "Tink says, at this rate, spring will be over by the time we get to Neverland. Look. Use your arms like this."

I spread my arms wide, like Peter had done. I flew straight and much, *much* faster, zipping past the Neverlanders easily.

The wind in my hair felt cold and delicious. "Awesome!"

Peter flew up beside me. "You have small strings streaming from your feet," he said matter-of-factly.

"Oh, right—my shoelaces." I had *really* been hurrying.

Afraid of losing my sneakers somewhere in the clouds, I landed on a roof with clay tiles and moonlight reflecting off the TV satellite dish. "This will just take a minute," I said, tying my shoes and double-knotting them as fast as I could.

"What are these funny things?"

I looked up from my feet.

Peter was walking a power line like a tightrope.

I gasped. "Be careful! Electricity can kill you."

That was a mistake. Telling Peter something is dangerous only makes him want to do it *more*.

"A new foe!" Peter cried, jumping up and drawing his golden sword eagerly.

I zoomed off the roof and flew between Peter and the power lines before he could take a swing at them.

"You can't fight it, Peter!" I said. Even Tink started chirping nervously, tugging at the leaves on Peter's shirt to hold him back.

"Don't worry, Wendy girl. I'll protect you." Peter pointed his sword at the power lines. "Have at thee, villain!"

I thought quickly. "I mean, it wouldn't be *right* for you to attack. You see, the electricity is already imprisoned."

That made Peter pause. "Imprisoned?"

I nodded solemnly, secretly very relieved. "Kept captive in those wires. It would be beneath your honor to attack it."

Peter liked this idea. He raised his chin and sheathed his sword with a flourish, looking very noble. "Come on, then."

He zoomed straight up, the little fairy flying in front of him. With a sigh of relief, I spread my arms and rushed after them.

Below us, the streets glinted silver in the moonlight. The leafless trees swayed a little in the wind, and

Christmas lights glittered on every block. Most of the houses were as small as my palm. As we rose higher in the dark blue sky, I noticed a bigger building with a familiar playground. "Hey, there's my school!"

"Look!" Peter said, pointing at a flock of geese flying just beside us. I don't think the birds were used to sharing the skies with kids and fairies. Hearing Peter, they scattered, honking in distress, and Tink let out a bell-like trill, a lot like a giggle.

Even higher, the streets started to look like a web of dark lines. I could only tell where the cars were by the white ovals their headlights made on the road. Peter led us higher still.

Soon, we were flying over the town. It was only a cluster of little lights below us. "That's exactly how it looks from a plane," I called to Peter, but then I remembered that my parents were somewhere down there, probably still at the party at Mom's firm. It occurred to me that Mom might not like me leaving without permission, but since that wasn't a very happy thought, I pushed it out of my mind.

If Mom and Dad could stay out late at parties, then I could definitely go to Neverland to have a few adventures. They were going to be busy anyway. They probably wouldn't even miss me, as long as I came back by Christmas.

With the thought of Neverland steady in my mind,

the fizzy feeling in my stomach became a hurricane of bubbles, tickling me so much that I giggled out loud. I flew so fast that the wind chilled me inside my jacket.

We passed through the clouds, and then we flew higher again, where the sky was blacker and dotted with little stars. They seemed a lot closer than they looked from the ground, and even though I couldn't prove it, I think they moved when I wasn't watching, rearranging themselves into different patterns.

"Wanna race?" I called to Peter as I zoomed past him. Technically, since I was already ahead of him when I asked, I kind of cheated. But I don't think Peter minded. He thrust his face against the wind with a wide grin, and the next time I looked, he was gaining on me steadily.

As soon as he was close enough, Peter shouted something. I didn't understand what he said, but he sounded half exasperated and half amused. (It's easy for me to recognize that tone. That's usually how Mom talks to me.)

I slowed and waited for him. "What?"

"Where are you going, Wendy girl? You don't even know the way," he said with a stern look.

"Oh." I looked at the big open sky. "How *do* you get to Neverland?"

Peter pointed ahead. "Second star on the right, and straight on to morning."

Those didn't sound like the most *exact* directions in the world. I wondered if I should have gone to the computer before we left and printed out a map, like Mom does before we go on a road trip. But then again, I had the feeling that the internet didn't know the way to Neverland.

"I guess I'll let you lead the way then," I said with a grin. When Peter sped off ahead of me, Tink zipped past too, right behind Peter.

Then we flew, all in a line. And flew some more.

After about the millionth star, it felt a lot like flying in a plane—a little bit boring if you don't have anything to do. I pulled my book out of my backpack and started doing a little research on Neverland.

The stars on that part of the Milky Way weren't very close, not close enough to give off enough light to read. But Tink did. And luckily, I was flying right behind her, my book open and tilted to catch her glow.

Personally, I thought this was pretty smart. It worked out great . . . at least until Peter glanced over his shoulder to check if I was still following.

He saw what I was doing and laughed. "Well, no Wendy girl has done *that* before. *Or* any of the Lost Boys."

Then Tink noticed me using her as a lamp. She *didn't* think it was funny. She chattered at me angrily.

"Sorry, Tink!" I cried, stuffing my book in my bag

next to Mom's iPod. "I didn't think that you would mind."

She just hissed. Then, she began zigzagging around Peter, so her light threw strange shadows everywhere.

If I worked harder to win Tink over, maybe she wouldn't get mad at me all the time, which would definitely make traveling more pleasant. In my reading, I'd learned that the fairy was a little vain, so I started with compliments.

"That's a very nice dress," I told her, pointing at the rose petals she wore.

Tink didn't chime, or turn toward me, or even stop zigzagging. I wasn't sure if she'd heard me.

"Did you make it yourself?" I asked, a little louder. "The dress, I mean?"

Instead of answering, or even acknowledging me, the little fairy zoomed straight ahead, way out of earshot.

"Is she always like that?" I asked Peter, feeling a little hurt.

"She is to the Wendy girls," Peter explained. "She hated the original Wendy, and I think she decided to hate the rest of you on principle."

"Oh," I said, disappointed. Then I straightened my shoulders and said, mostly to myself, "I'll just have to work extra hard to win her over."

"Right," Peter said, his mouth quirking at the

corners. He didn't think it was possible, but he was humoring me—I get that a lot, too.

I couldn't wait to prove him wrong.

It turned out that I didn't really *need* Mom's iPod to keep me entertained during the trip. After the book incident, Peter and Tink came up with plenty of stuff to do while we were traveling.

Soaring ahead of us, Tink plucked something from the air above her head and threw it to Peter.

"Here!" Peter said, and tossed it to me.

I caught it and took a good look—it was a glowing sphere, smaller than the fairy but much, much brighter. It warmed my palm, and when I opened my hand a little wider, it twinkled merrily. "What is it?"

"A baby star," Peter said, like this was obvious.

I wondered if it was a good idea to use a star as a landmark if they moved around like that, but I didn't say so. "It's not as big as they tell us in school."

"*Grown-ups.* They don't know *anything*," Peter said scornfully. He zipped forward. "I'm ready!"

I threw the star to Tink, who passed it to Peter. He let it drop, almost all the way to the clouds, before he swooped down and snatched it up.

He was definitely showing off, but I was still pretty impressed.

The next time he threw it to me, I let it fall for a few seconds before I rushed down and caught it—but

I stubbed my toe on the moon, which was soccer ball sized and half hidden in the clouds.

Tink made a high-pitched ring, kind of like a really annoying telephone, her arms wrapped around her middle. I was pretty sure she was laughing.

Tossing the star back to Peter, I hung my head, my face so hot that I was surprised that it didn't glow as brightly as the fairy's.

Peter watched me, frowning a little. I couldn't tell what he was thinking, but I was afraid he would tell me that it served me right for being such a copycat.

But all he said was "Pretty good for a first try. Next time, dive with your hands first. You'll be able to see where you're going."

That made me feel better.

I kept throwing the star to Tink, hoping she might get friendlier, but she never threw it to me. We had to stop when we reached a second star, a bigger one who turned snobbishly away when it saw us. As we went, the baby star bobbed a little in the air, like it was waving good-bye, before shooting home.

Then Peter demonstrated some midflight acrobatics. I'd been taking gymnastics for years, and being able to fly made everything *so* much easier. When he did three somersaults, I did three too.

"Not bad, Wendy girl," Peter said with a small smirk. "But can you do this?"

He did four cartwheels in a row in a circle around me, even while I was flying.

Then I tried. I definitely counted four cartwheels, but unfortunately, I didn't pay attention to where my feet were going. My ankle smacked into the little fairy, almost knocking her out of the sky.

"Oops!" I straightened up quickly as she chattered angrily at me, shaking one fist and smoothing her hair down with her other hand. "Sorry, Tink! I didn't see you there."

Peter didn't seem to be bothered. "Bet you can't do *this*."

He did a cartwheel, a round-off, and a backflip, all in a row.

I grinned. I knew I could do it. Once, I'd even done it when I *wasn't* flying. So, I did a cartwheel, a round-off, and *two* backflips.

That might have been a mistake too. Either Peter didn't like me outdoing him, or he got sick of practicing acrobatics for some other reason.

Lying with his hands behind his head, like he was floating backward, Peter started telling me about his adventures—about feeding Captain Hook's hand to the crocodile, and rescuing Princess Tiger Lily from the pirates, and bringing the Lost Boys a mother. . . .

Maybe it was the time of day, or the fact that I had reread some of his stories an hour or so before, but my eyelids began to droop. Before long, I fell asleep. This was a problem, because apparently, when you aren't awake, you might stop flying. Peter had to fly down and catch me. I woke up dangling from his hands, my toes brushing the Milky Way below.

Tink pulled my hair. "Oww!" I said, swatting at her sleepily.

She dodged and chittered angrily.

"What did she say?" I asked.

"That you just wanted to hold my hand," Peter said.

I snatched my hand back, starting to blush. "Tink, I already told you. I don't *like* like Peter. It's just—I'm usually asleep by now."

The fairy chimed in a scornful way, but Peter showed me how to stretch out on a strong gust of wind, which would keep me moving in the right direction even while I was sleeping. I started to thank him, but then he said, "None of the *other* Wendy girls fell asleep listening to me talk."

"Sorry," I murmured. Silently wondering if maybe the other Wendy girls were just better at *pretending* to listen to Peter, I drifted off to sleep.

"Wendy girl, wake up!" A hand shook me roughly.

I opened my eyes sleepily and saw the stars above me, and I remembered that I was riding the back of the wind with Peter Pan. I sat up with a start. Someone had tucked a bit of cloud around me as I slept, and I knew it wasn't Tink. I smiled, liking Peter a little more.

"Time for a rest stop?" I said, rubbing my eyes. The air smelled like saltwater.

Peter shook his head and stretched lazily, but when he looked ahead, he started to grin, almost in spite of himself. "It's Neverland."

4 Something Eats Mom's iPod

"We get off here," Peter said.

Even the air was different in Neverland. It had a taste, both familiar and exciting at once, like the first bite of ice cream on the first day of summer. When you breathed it in, you started to feel like you do on that day, with school months and months away. My toes and fingers tingled in a strange way, and anything felt possible.

We glided over the water toward Neverland. The sun hadn't risen yet, but it was getting ready to. The sky glowed a little, and I could see the island rising up like a mountain out of the sea, practically covered in a lush forest. Beaches circled it like white ribbon. The cliffs above them shone gold in the predawn light.

"How beautiful!" I exclaimed. It was so warm that I peeled off my jacket and stuffed it into my backpack. A couple of dolphins surfaced close to shore, making *chee-chee-chee* noises with toothy grins, like they were welcoming us. Flamingos took flight as we passed.

"What are those lights?" I asked, pointing to a huge tree that stood alone, at the edge of a cliff. They winked on and off among the leaves—little white and blue and purplish flashes. "Are they fireflies?"

Tink screeched. Peter didn't bother to translate, but I knew that she hadn't said anything nice. I think she might have still been upset about me kicking her during those cartwheels.

"Those are fairies," Peter said, sounding a little bored. Apparently, I wasn't the *only* visitor who asked that question. "They're just now waking up."

We flew past another cove. The indigo water there was dotted with boulders. On each rock sat at least one figure with a glittering tail that curved toward the sea. The mermaids' hair fell past their waists, in all different colors—blond and blue, black with shades of violet or green, a coppery sort of red.

"Is that Mermaids' Lagoon? How lovely! There are so many of them!" I counted. "Twenty, at least. Are they combing their hair?"

"They have to. Fish swim through it at night. You should see what a mess they are when they can't find their combs. The tangles get as big and round as a Never bird nest." Peter laughed at the thought.

The mermaids sang as they combed. In the dim light, it sounded low and eerie.

"Who's that one sitting on the rock a little higher than the others?"

"That's Maris, queen of the mermaids."

When she saw us fly across their bay, her eyes narrowed.

We circled the lagoon. We flew so close that I could see the lime green highlights in the queen's blond hair, and I waved. The mermaids watched Peter, all their heads turning at once.

I waved harder, thinking that they couldn't see me. "Hello!"

Only one of the mermaids, the littlest one, waved back. The mermaid queen grabbed her arm and pulled her under the waves. The other mermaids followed them, their tails throwing up spray.

"Mermaids *aren't* friendly," Peter told me. "They'll drag you under if you let them."

"Well, I'm going to make friends with one," I told Peter matter-of-factly.

Tink gave a gleeful chirp and then pressed her hands over her mouth, as if she was trying to keep herself from cheering.

Peter stared at me, eyes wide with horror. Actually, he looked exactly how I felt when he told me that he was going to fight the power lines.

"I'm serious," he said. "I've rescued more than one Wendy girl from drowning."

Underwater, the mermaids continued their eerie song, humming instead of singing, louder and louder. The water just below us continued to bubble, and as I watched, a giant wave started to grow—five feet, ten feet, twenty.

"Uh-oh," I said, zipping out of the way right before it crashed. Peter dodged in time too, but Tink got soaked.

Sputtering, she fell through the air. Two mermaids— one with black hair and one with green—surfaced, arms outstretched, webbed fingers spread, ready to catch the tiny fairy. The mermaids' lips curled up, showing a glimmer of teeth.

"Fairy dust doesn't work when it's wet," Peter told me offhandedly as he swooped down and caught Tink a few feet from the water.

The mermaids hissed at him and slid back under the ocean.

"See what I mean?" Peter told me, placing Tink on his shoulder as she waited impatiently for her fairy dust to dry. "Not friend material."

"I still think they're lovely," I said stubbornly, even more determined to find one and become friends, but I knew better than to say so. It *would* be a little trickier than I expected. In the meantime, I decided to try befriending the humans on the island first. *They* couldn't send a giant wave at me before we'd introduced ourselves. "Do you know where Tiger Lily is?"

"In there," Peter said, gesturing loftily to the forest that covered most of the island.

I guessed that meant *no*.

"You know, she's really not very friendly either. She likes me, of course. And some of the Lost Boys. Usually not the Wendy girls."

I snorted softly to myself. Peter made it sound like *everyone* hated me.

We flew quickly around the rest of the island. I think that was Peter's way of giving me a tour. Even the trees were different. They were much bigger than the ones at home—some of their trunks were as wide as I was tall. Their dark waxy leaves grew in all different sizes—from a few as small as my pinky toe to some as big as my dad—even on the same tree.

Then a ship emerged from one of the coves. The flag tied to its mast had a skull and bones, and its sails were red. *Jolly Roger* was painted on the side in faded white letters.

I gasped. "Is that the pirate ship?"

Peter's eyes glittered, and for the first time, he looked a little dangerous. "Would you like an adventure now, or would you like to meet the Lost Boys first?"

"Now, please," I said quickly.

He grinned, pointing down to the deck of the ship. "There's Hook."

The captain of the *Jolly Roger* hadn't seen us yet. He strolled slowly up to the bow, smoking a cigar. He wore an old-fashioned coat with gold trim and a black hat with a long, fluffy feather. His shirt had ruffles, and his curly black hair was even longer than Mom's. A chubby pirate lit him a second cigar. One of the other pirates slept on deck, curled up with a bit of rope for a teddy bear. Hook kicked him as he passed.

From Peter's shoulder, Tink chimed in.

Peter made a face. "She says we don't have time to kill Captain Hook."

"There has to be something we can do," I said thoughtfully. "I know!" Then I whispered my plan in his ear.

Pan liked the idea so much that he crowed. All the pirates looked up at once, searching the sky.

"There! There!" Captain Hook shouted, pointing straight at Peter. "Ready Long Tom!"

I turned to Peter to ask what Long Tom was, but Peter had already started flying toward the pirates. "I'll be right back," he told me. He swooped down to the *Jolly Roger*, his golden sword drawn. "Greetings, Hook!" he cried.

Passing over the deck, Peter sliced through Hook's belt with one stroke, and the captain's trousers fell, exposing underpants with little hearts on them.

"What are you laughing at?" Hook shouted at his crew, who stopped mid-ha. "Shoot him!"

I couldn't just wait around and let Peter have all the fun. This was supposed to be *my* first adventure, after all. Grinning with excitement, I flew in after him.

"Good morning," I told the captain brightly, and snatched his hat off.

The whole right side of his head was one big scar. His ear was completely gone. It was so ugly that I almost stopped flying to get a closer look, but then I noticed three pirates running toward me with their swords raised. I zipped quickly out of reach—to where Peter stood, lounging against a low cloud, the way that normal people might lean against a wall.

Tink tugged the hat out of my hands and dropped it ceremoniously on Peter's head, arranging the long feather just so.

Peter stood up a little straighter and crowed again. "How clever I am!" he said, hands on his hips, watching the commotion on the *Jolly Roger* with glee.

Hook covered his scar with his one good hand, trying to keep the pirates from staring at it. "What happened to his ear?" I asked.

"The crocodile got another nibble," Peter said wickedly.

I shuddered, which only made Peter smile even wider.

"Return that hat at once, you insolent youth," the captain shouted at Peter, shaking his hook.

The curved metal glinted cruelly in the growing light. I gulped, but Peter only shouted back, "Never, you codfish!" To me, he asked, "What does *insolent* mean?"

I didn't know. Back home, I had a computer for this sort of question. So, I guessed. "I'm sure it's a compliment."

"Tink couldn't tell me either," Peter said with a deep, sad sigh.

"Prepare to meet your end, boy!" Hook shouted. He moved quickly out of the way, revealing a cylinder-shaped object made out of black iron, longer than I was tall.

"Uh-oh," I said. "Is that a cannon?"

Tink started chittering anxiously. The pirates around the cannon leered, showing missing teeth. Peter just stood tall in front of the cloud. Slowly, tauntingly, he crossed his eyes and stuck out his tongue.

"Fire!" cried Hook.

"Incoming!" shouted Peter.

Something black and round blasted out of the cannon with a puff of smoke.

Maybe Peter and Tink were used to cannonballs, but *I* certainly wasn't.

I barrel-rolled out of the way, holding on to the straps of my backpack so I wouldn't lose it. A few seconds later, the cannonball fell into the ocean with a comforting *thunk*. Still tumbling, I let out the breath I'd been holding.

"That was close," I told Peter, righting myself. My heart was still beating pretty hard.

Peter suddenly pointed. "Something fell out of your bag."

I looked down. A rectangular glint of silver was dropping toward the ocean. "Oh, no—Mom's iPod!"

I raced it to the water, arms stretched out to grab it. If I lost it, there was no way I could keep from getting in trouble when I went home. I almost rescued it—I came close enough to hear "Jingle Bells" playing. Ten feet from the water, my fingertips brushed it, and I reached just a little farther.

But then huge jaws, lined with foot-long teeth, rose from the water and snapped up Mom's iPod.

5
I Try to Be a Mother

I screamed and shot away from the water, zipping over to where Peter was waiting.

"What *was* that?" I asked, hiding behind Peter. The monster swam over a huge wave toward the pirates, all the teeth visible in its enormous jaws.

"Croc, the crocodile," he said, like I should know.

"You dogs!" Hook shouted to his men on the ship. "Ready the cannon *again*!"

"It's as big as a dinosaur!" I said.

The monster slithered around the *Jolly Roger* lazily. The only parts of him visible above the water were the dark green ridges on his back and his yellow, bulblike eyes. He *was* huge—about two-thirds the length of the ship.

Then Croc rose from the sea and clawed at the ship's rail. Seeing his old enemy, Captain Hook screamed so loudly that the sound echoed off Neverland's cliffs.

"Raise anchor, lads!" a chubby pirate shouted. "Unlash the sails!"

"What's that long scar?" I asked. It ran from right above the crocodile's eye all the way down to his tail.

"War wound," Peter said. "Compliments of Hook."

Since he couldn't get over the rail, Croc sank slowly back into the ocean. The pirates tried to aim the cannon at him, but the reptile sank out of sight.

The fairy chirped something to Peter.

"Tink's right," he said, tossing his head so that the feather bounced in an eye-catching way. "We should go. It won't be any fun to bother the pirates while the crocodile's here."

"But what about the iPod?" I said.

Tink said something with a smug smile, and Peter nodded solemnly. "Looks like it's gone forever."

He started flying back toward the island, and I flew after him, worrying about home. Mom was going to be really mad.

"It wasn't mine."

But Peter spoke before I could explain about Mom.

"What *is* an iPod?" he asked.

"It plays music."

"I can do that." Peter pulled some wooden pipes out of his pocket—hollow reeds dried out, cut to different lengths, and tied together flat with very slender vines. He started to blow a merry tune. He watched me eagerly, like he wanted me to say that he was much better than anything that had just gotten eaten by a crocodile.

I smiled a little. Peter's playing wasn't exactly the same, and it definitely wouldn't keep me from getting in trouble for losing Mom's iPod. But it was nice of him to try. Just as nice as covering me with a cloud blanket while I slept.

From Peter's shoulder, Tink chimed something, interrupting his tune, and he took the pipes away from his mouth. "Look! There are the Lost Boys now. And Tiger Lily."

"Where?" I asked excitedly, and Peter pointed to a clearing below us.

I saw Tiger Lily first—her chin held high, her long black hair braided with feathers, the beaded diamond pattern stitched on her deerskin dress. She *looked* like a princess should look, tall and proud and royal. The Lost Boys gathered around her, all leaning forward, like they were listening intently.

None of them looked up, and no one looked all that excited to make a new friend. I started to feel awkward.

Like maybe nobody wanted me in Neverland.

Then Peter crowed as loud as he could to get their attention.

All the Lost Boys turned at once. Then they waved wildly, crying, "Peter! Peter!" and once, "Hey, it's the Wendy girl!"

Tiger Lily looked too. When I thought she glanced my way, I tried to wave at her, but she must not have seen. She turned and disappeared into the trees.

My shyness didn't get any better after Peter and I landed.

"What a hat, Peter!" cried one Lost Boy.

"Is it Hook's?"

"Of course it's Hook's," said Peter.

"Can I try it?" asked another Lost Boy.

I'd landed a little bit behind Peter and was waiting for him to introduce me. My stomach was in knots. Standing there, I wasn't at all sure that they wanted me to come.

"Later," Peter said, stepping aside, gesturing to me with both hands and a huge grin. "Lost Boys," he announced proudly, "I've brought you the latest Wendy girl."

The Lost Boys rushed forward, crowding around me, pressing very close. It was too much attention at once. I had to stop myself from taking a step back.

"My *name* is Ashley," I said, hoping that the Lost

Boys wouldn't call me Wendy girl all the time the way Peter did.

No such luck.

"Hi, Wendy girl!" said the second-shortest one. His hair was just as curly as Peter's, but a whiter shade of blond. "I'm Dibs!"

Another boy pushed Dibs out of the way. He was almost as tall as I was, and his dark hair was a little long. His pants looked like bell-bottoms. He had obviously been in Neverland for a while. "Prank," he said, shaking my hand heartily.

"I'm Button," said a slow, bashful voice. It belonged to the shyest of the Lost Boys, the one standing to the side and shuffling his feet. It was obvious where he got his name. He had hundreds of buttons sewn to his shirt, straining against the ragged fabric. (He was a little chubbier than the rest.)

"Hi, Button," I said. At least they were much friendlier than Tink. *And* Peter, actually.

"And that's Kyle," Peter said, pointing to the little boy hiding behind Button.

"Kyle?" I repeated, surprised. I mean, I had a Kyle in my class two years ago. After *Dibs* and *Prank* and *Button*, *Kyle* seemed like a pretty ordinary name.

The little boy scowled immediately, looking a lot like Peter did when he didn't like something. The Lost Boys were quick to defend him.

"He hasn't gotten a Neverland name yet."

"Why not?" I asked.

"He just got here."

"You should be grateful to Kyle," said Peter. *"He's* the one who kept saying we could use a Wendy girl to help out."

"Well, really, he was *nagging*," said one (Prank, I think), but the other two elbowed him hard.

"I didn't mean to insult anyone," I said quickly. "I've always liked the name Kyle." Then I leaned closer to the littlest Lost Boy, adding, "Actually, I *should* thank you for convincing Peter to go get me."

Kyle smiled at that. His front teeth were missing. It made me wonder how *long* his front teeth would be missing, if he didn't get any older.

I looked around for other Lost Boys waiting to be introduced, but nobody else was there. "Shouldn't there be *more* of you?" I *had* expected lots and lots of them.

"We lost a few recently," Prank said, looking a little nervous.

"They were growing up," Peter said darkly, and all the Lost Boys shuddered.

"What happened to them?" I asked, curious.

"Are you sure this is a Wendy girl, Peter?" asked Dibs.

Prank was suspicious too. "She certainly asks a lot of

questions. Wendy girls don't ask questions."

"Where's her nightgown?" Button said. "I thought all Wendy girls were supposed to have nightgowns."

I looked down at my pajamas. They were perfectly presentable. The neon pink and green stripes weren't even a little bit faded. "I haven't worn a nightgown since I was *eight*." It seemed weird that they wouldn't like me just because I slept in the wrong clothes.

"Well, *I* like her," said Kyle, giving all the other Lost Boys that fierce scowl. "Peter, what do you think?"

The Lost Boys all turned to their leader. Under Hook's hat, Peter regarded me shrewdly. "Well, she's not like any of the Wendy girls we've had in Neverland before, but I'm sure that she'll make a fine mother for you all."

"A mother!" chorused the Lost Boys, delighted.

"A mother?" I repeated. My stomach plummeted. I'd come to Neverland for adventure!

The Lost Boys crowded around me again, pressing so close that I couldn't tell who was saying what.

"Will you tell us stories?"

"Will you make us dinner?"

"Make us *cookies*?"

"Sew up our clothes?"

"Why does everyone think I can sew?" I asked, confused.

The Lost Boys obviously had really old-fashioned

ideas about girls. Maybe because they had been stuck in Neverland so long. It had been *decades* since Grandma Delaney had been the Wendy girl.

"You're our *mother*," said Dibs wistfully.

"I'm *eleven*," I told them.

"That's not a problem," Kyle said.

"It just takes a little Pretending," Button said.

"All of the Wendy girls were young," Prank added.

"It *is* a problem," I said. "I can't be anybody's mother. I won't have time to—" But I didn't get a chance to finish.

All the Lost Boys gasped at once, staring at me.

"But that's why you came, isn't it?" Dibs said finally. "Peter brought you to be our mother, didn't he?"

I had come to Neverland to be their *friend*, not their mom, but it wasn't my opinion they wanted.

One by one, the Lost Boys and Tink turned to Peter.

"Maybe you're right, Tink," Peter said, looking at me. The feather on Hook's hat fell in front of his face, and he pushed it aside hastily. "If she doesn't want to be our mother, she isn't much use to us. Maybe I *should* take her back."

I'd just gotten to Neverland. I couldn't leave *now*. I hadn't even gotten a chance to talk to the mermaids. Or Tiger Lily.

I thought quickly. There had to be a way out of this. Then I hung my head and shuffled my feet like I was moping. "It's not that I don't *want* to be your mother. I just don't think that I can."

"Sure, you can," Button said encouragingly.

"All Wendy girls can be mothers!" Dibs said.

"But I'm not sure that you would like it," I said with a heavy sigh. "Mothers today are different. Not what you're expecting."

"We'll love it!"

"Please, Wendy girl," Dibs said.

I looked at him for a long minute, weighing the decision.

I definitely had a plan, but tricking the Lost Boys wasn't the best way to start our friendship. Then again, I *knew* being their mother was all wrong, even if they didn't know it yet. They had no idea how much fun our adventures could be if I wasn't stuck being a mother. They would all forgive me as soon as they found out.

Finally, reluctantly, I nodded.

The Lost Boys raised a cheer. Even Peter smiled. Only Tink had doubts. She flew up to the branch above me, watching me through narrowed eyes.

"First things first," I said. "To be a mother, I need some paper."

"Paper?" Prank repeated, confused.

"Not the apron?" Dibs said. "You mean the apron, right?"

"Dibs, get your mother paper!" Peter ordered. Dibs

scurried over to a birch tree and started ripping off long strips of bark.

"And glasses," I added.

"I'll do it!" said Button, and he began gathering twigs and handfuls of grass.

"And I'll need a computer," I said firmly.

The Lost Boys all looked at each other, puzzled.

"A *what?*" Prank said.

"Computers are banned from Neverland," Peter said in his most commanding voice. It made me think that he didn't know what one was.

"Okay, just the paper and glasses, then," I said quickly, ready to get it over with.

Dibs dropped the bark in my lap, which actually did look like paper, and Button ceremoniously presented me with the glasses he had made—twigs bound together with long grasses.

"Wow," I said, impressed. "This is really something, Button."

Button beamed. "I got our mother's first compliment."

The expressions of all the other boys darkened, instantly jealous. I had no idea that making a comment would have that kind of reaction. Sometimes, back home, I had trouble just getting someone to take me seriously.

I smiled a little. The Lost Boys turned to me with eager looks.

"Will you make us cookies?" asked Prank.

"Will you tuck us in, Mother?" said Kyle.

I put the glasses on and stood up very straight, the same way Mom does before she goes to an important meeting. "In a minute," I told the Lost Boys, and marched over to the other side of the clearing. The boys followed me and watched as I spread my papers out on a large rock, pretending it was a desk.

They watched me spread them out and stack them up three times more before Peter lost patience. "Tell us a story, Mother!" he said.

"Yes, tell us a story," said Dibs.

I didn't look at them, but I stood up, flipping through the bark in my hands like I was reading quickly. "You'll have to wait a little while longer," I said, walking across the clearing to another rock. "I'm almost done."

Peter scowled. *"Now."*

Dibs took it up next, saying, "Now, now, now." The rest of the boys started chanting it and stomping around me. "Now, now, now, now."

I looked at them all sternly. "Boys, this is very important work that Mommy's doing. You won't understand it until you're older."

"But we're not going to get any older," Button said doubtfully.

"I don't have time for this," I said, standing back up and straightening my shoulders the way Mom does when Dad says something she doesn't like.

They stared at me as I stormed across the clearing again.

"You aren't any good at this mothering business," said Prank flatly.

"She did try to tell us," Kyle reminded everyone. "She *said* mothers are different."

"Mom said all of those things to me just this Monday," I admitted.

"You *can't* be our mother. Not like that," Peter said.

Slowly, I took off the glasses, looking at the ground and trying not to seem too triumphant.

I didn't mention that Mom didn't *usually* say things like that. She usually put her work aside until I went to bed. I also didn't mention that Mom had apologized on Tuesday morning for what she said.

I imagined how she would look if she had seen me acting this way, and then I really *did* feel ashamed. She was never this bad.

But I didn't feel so guilty that I gave in.

"Can we keep her anyway?" Kyle said.

"We've never had a Wendy girl who wasn't a mother before," Prank said uncertainly.

"We *need* a mother," said Dibs, putting his fists on his hips like Peter. "Get another Wendy girl."

"Let's *please* keep her," Button said to Peter. "I like her."

"And I've never had a Wendy girl before," Kyle reminded him.

I held my breath. If I went home, the weekend would be even bleaker and more boring that it had seemed the night before (especially since Mom would probably punish me for losing her iPod).

Peter had his shrewd, judging look on. It couldn't mean anything *good*. Then he started to pace, the hat's feather bobbing behind him. After a second, Dibs paced too, a couple feet behind Peter.

Tink chirped impatiently.

"I guess we have to," Peter said finally. The Lost Boys and I cheered, but then he added, "We need a girl around for the spring cleaning. You boys could use the help. That's what Kyle's been saying, after all."

I had forgotten about spring cleaning. I still wasn't completely sold on the idea.

I mean, this was *Neverland*. I wanted to go meet mermaids and explore the island, not dust or sweep or whatever. But I had barely gotten away with not being their mother. So, if all I needed to do to keep Peter from taking me home was a few chores, then I would definitely do it.

"Absolutely," I said quickly. "Let me just get something before we start."

6
The Lost Boys Get Their Portraits Taken

When I took the camera out of my backpack, hoping to take some good pictures while I was working, all of the Lost Boys stared. Even Peter peered around their heads curiously.

The Neverlanders were fascinated by technology, but they didn't really understand it very well.

"What is it?" Button asked.

I blinked, surprised. I would've never guessed that Peter and the Lost Boys didn't know what a camera was.

"It's my dad's camera," I explained.

"What does a camera *do*?" asked Dibs, eyeing it nervously.

"It takes your picture. This one's special. It'll give you a photo right away. Here, let me show you. Peter first." When the bulb flashed, Peter jumped away so quickly that Hook's hat fell off.

I could see the image on the little screen in the back of the camera, but the others couldn't. With a whirring sound, the picture started coming out at the bottom in short jerks as it printed. The Lost Boys gathered around to look at it.

"It's just a little piece of paper," Peter said shortly.

"Wait for it to come out." The green of the leaves above Peter showed up first, and then his hat. The Lost Boys oohed and aahed. Then Peter himself appeared in the photo—his eyes, then his nose, and then his mouth, scowling slightly. When the picture finished printing and fell out, we could see Peter's whole image, even his fists on his hips.

"There you are!" I said triumphantly.

Peter glared at the photo. He was on the verge of not liking it.

"Oh, Peter," I said quickly, before he decided to overreact and ban cameras from Neverland forever. "You look dashing. Fearsome, even. No wonder the pirates are scared of you."

That won him over. Peter picked up the hat again and drew his sword. "Another one," he demanded.

After Peter had a half a dozen pictures of himself, everyone else wanted one too, even Tink. She never did figure out what a photograph was. She propped hers against a rock and started fussing with her hair.

"It's not a mirror," I told her, trying to explain.

She hissed at me, fluttering her wings angrily. Then she hugged the Polaroid photo to her chest (it looked poster-sized on her) and zipped through the trees and out of sight, like she thought I was going to steal her picture.

Just the tiniest bit of doubt nagged at me. Maybe Tink and I would *never* be friends.

Kyle tugged on my pajamas. "One more? With me and Button together?"

Smiling, I raised the camera again.

Two minutes after I started worrying that I would run out of film, the Lost Boys took a break to admire their photos, sitting on a pile of blankets and passing pictures around the same way some of my classmates pass around baseball cards at recess. I sat with them, glad that the camera was such a hit.

"I look like Peter," Dibs said. He pushed a photo of himself in my face. "Wendy girl, don't I look like Peter?"

"No," Peter said coldly, but you know, I did kind of see the resemblance.

"There has to be something we can do with these," Prank said, frowning in concentration. "Something really good."

I didn't know what he meant, so I said slowly, "We

could make an album or something."

"He means a trick," Button told me. "Prank likes to play tricks on people."

"Prank, can I help this time?" Kyle said.

Dibs snatched up Button's picture and shoved *that* in my face. "Look how big Button's cheeks are. What a fatso."

"That's not very nice!" I told him fiercely.

So far, Dibs was definitely my least favorite Lost Boy.

Seeing Button look down with an embarrassed frown, I added stoutly, "Besides, they say that the camera adds ten pounds." That was what my mother always said when she thought that she looked fat in a picture.

All the Lost Boys gasped, horrified, and Tink shrieked loudly, emerging from the leaves right above their heads. Even Peter seemed alarmed. They all stared at the camera with new respect.

"What?" I said, distracted by the way Tink was touching her hips, her arms, her knees, as if reassuring herself that they hadn't changed.

"You've taken so many pictures," Button said, looking at the pile of Polaroids.

"That's"— Prank paused, counting on his fingers— "a million trillion pounds!"

"It doesn't *really* add ten pounds. It only looks like it in the picture," I said, but the Lost Boys just stared at their hands, as if waiting for them to swell.

"Could we take pictures of the pirates?" Prank asked, grinning broadly. "Maybe we could make them so big that it would sink the *Jolly Roger*. How many pictures would that take?"

"It only *looks* like it adds ten pounds," I repeated, exasperated.

I could tell Tink didn't believe me, but she had a reason to be worried. Adding ten pounds to someone as small as she was would make her eight times heavier.

Suddenly, Tink smiled one of her most evil smiles and chirped something to Peter. I'd known her long enough to start to worry.

"I suppose you're right, Tink. We should really get started on our spring cleaning if we want to be finished before bedtime," Peter said, turning to me.

The photo shoot had been fun while it lasted.

"Fine," I said wearily. "Where's your mop?"

The Lost Boys exchanged glances. "We don't have any of those," Button said.

"I'm not supposed to use my toothbrush, am I?" I had seen people cleaning with their toothbrushes in movies.

"What's a toothbrush?" Dibs asked, which made me worry that the Lost Boys needed a dentist more than a mother.

"I don't think it would help," Kyle told me.

"It's not that kind of spring cleaning," said Button.

"Then what are we cleaning?" I said, starting to feel more hopeful about the whole business.

The boys all pointed at once—straight up.

I looked. The tree sparkled a little in the bright afternoon light. "Are you waiting for all the leaves to fall off? Because it's the wrong season."

"We have a Never bird problem," Button said solemnly.

"They migrated back a few days ago," Dibs explained, "and they've already built their nests."

I couldn't understand where the Never birds were *supposed* to be building their nests if not in Neverland trees, but then Kyle complained, "I've had to sleep on the ground for two whole nights."

"They keep chasing us out," Prank said glumly. "We can barely get *near* our beds."

I looked again at the ragged blankets scattered around the tree's trunk. "Oh, you *live* up there."

"She's not the smartest Wendy girl we've ever had," Peter explained to the Lost Boys apologetically.

"Hey!" I cried, insulted.

"The Never birds chase all of us out," Kyle told me.

"All except Peter," said Dibs with a proud smile.

"Naturally," said Peter, raising Hook's hat and bowing extravagantly.

"Well, how many birds are we talking about?" I asked, imagining hundreds.

The Lost Boys looked at each other and didn't answer. "We didn't count," Button said.

"They're big," said Prank.

"Bigger than me!" Kyle said, and when my eyes widened, he added, "Well, with their wings spread anyway."

"Huge beaks," said Button.

"And claws as long as your hand!" Prank said.

Dibs rolled his eyes. "Not *that* long."

Kyle and Button both squirmed, glancing up at the tree fearfully, but Peter, Prank, and Dibs didn't look scared at all. They kind of looked the way I felt when Dad asked me to rake up all the leaves in the backyard. To them, Never bird relocation was a time-consuming chore that they were more than happy to pass off to someone else, like their new Wendy girl.

I didn't know if I should feel nervous or resentful.

"I guess someone better show me," I said.

"Not it!" Dibs shouted.

"Not it!" shouted Prank and Button, and a half second later, Tink chimed in too. I turned to Peter, who pointed to Kyle.

"Careful," Button said. "They've got a nasty bite."

I gulped.

7
I Meet the Never Birds

"*I*f they're dangerous, why are you sending me with the littlest one?" I asked Peter. It seemed like, if anyone was coming with me, it should be Peter. *He* had a sword.

"I'm not little!" cried Kyle. He shot upward into the trees, scowling fiercely.

"Now you've done it," Prank said, shaking his head.

"Hurt his feelings," Button said sympathetically.

"I didn't mean it like *that*," I said with a deep sigh. Even making friends with the Lost Boys was turning out to be harder than I'd thought.

I flew up after Kyle, taking the camera with me.

Since I'd already lost Mom's iPod, I really had to take care of Dad's camera, or *both* parents would be mad at me as soon as I got home.

Kyle was perched on a slender branch pretty close to the top. He stared intently at something one branch above him.

"Kyle, I'm sor—," I started.

He pressed a finger to his lips, signaling me to be quiet. "Don't wake it up."

"Wake up what?"

"The Never bird! It's right there. Five feet from you."

I looked nervously. "I don't see anything," I whispered, beginning to worry that maybe Never birds were invisible, at least to people who hadn't been in Neverland for more than a few hours. I wondered if I should pretend to see it, just in case they really would send me home if I turned out to be unhelpful with the Never birds as well.

Kyle pointed. "Right there."

I saw the nest first, and then a slight movement right above it—every time the bird breathed.

"Oh," I said, relieved. The bird was *completely* camouflaged. It looked exactly like the tree trunk, right down to the dappled gray color and the pattern of the bark.

"There's a green one over there," Kyle said, pointing

to the nest in the branch to our right.

That bird's feathers were as green as the leaves around it.

"It blends in!" I cried, delighted. "Like a chameleon!" It was so cool that I couldn't resist taking a picture.

The flash woke the Never bird. It noticed us with a squawk and launched itself in our direction. Kyle and I zipped out of the tree so fast that I almost dropped the camera. (So much for taking good care of it.)

Once we were gone, the Never bird returned to her nest, all her leaf-colored feathers still ruffled angrily.

"Maybe I should've turned the flash off," I whispered to Kyle, breathing hard.

"Peter was right. You really aren't the smartest Wendy girl we've ever had," Prank said thoughtfully, rising into the air next to us.

I was getting *really* tired of people calling me stupid. "If you came up here just to insult me, you can go right back down," I told Prank coldly.

"Peter sent me to help you." It didn't sound like Prank was very happy about it.

"The Never birds are really hard to get out," Kyle said.

"Hard enough that maybe we should find you guys a new tree to live in?" I said, my heart still beating really fast. A Never bird's beak looks a lot bigger when it comes within a few inches of your face.

Kyle and Prank shook their heads sadly. Prank flew down into the trees. He pushed a few of the leaves out of the way to reveal a hammock bed hanging from the branch. It was made out of two leaves, the six-foot-long kind. The bottom leaf was waxy and flexible and full of battered blankets. Each end was secured to the branch with strong rope. Looking around, I saw three other hammock beds hanging from the branches around it.

I was impressed. I mean, back home, I just had a tree house. Peter, Tink, and the Lost Boys had a Tree *Home.*

The closest Never bird—just a few branches above us—squawked at Prank, ruffling its feathers threateningly.

"Watch—it's going to chase me out," Prank said, creeping closer to the bird. He didn't sound worried at all.

"Is it a good idea to tease it?" I asked, but as soon as the Never bird took flight and dived at Prank's head, he dived out of the tree.

"Same deal as last time," he said. "They're getting so predictable."

"We could move the beds," I suggested hopefully.

"Maybe, but we couldn't move Peter's house," Kyle said. He pointed upward.

High up, almost as high as the Never bird's nest, a little red house sat, lashed to a few sturdy branches. Lacy white curtains hung in the windows, and flowers grew on the roof. It didn't look like a house that Peter would pick out for himself.

"He's very attached to it," Kyle added.

"It's very old," Prank said. "From the time of the original Wendy."

"Maybe you could all sleep in there!" I said excitedly, hoping that I would get to see the inside, but the two Lost Boys shook their heads.

"We're not allowed in there," Kyle said.

"Well, what did you do last year?" I asked, beginning to worry that I would run out of ideas.

"Kicked the nests out of the tree, Never bird and all," Prank said with one of his wicked grins.

"But there could be eggs inside them!" I cried. "We can't do that!"

Prank looked a little disappointed, but he shrugged. "It was dangerous, anyway. One of the Never birds caught Button. He still has the scars."

I thought hard. I was determined to come up with a plan that would prove I wasn't the dumbest Wendy girl ever. "Have you ever tried luring them out with food?" I asked. "What do they eat anyway?"

"Lost Boys named Kyle," Prank said seriously.

Kyle went very still and very white. For a second, I

believed Prank, but then I caught the beginning of a smirk on his face.

"That's not true," I told Kyle, giving Prank a dirty look. "He's making it up to scare you."

"Well, we could try scaring them out," Prank said innocently. "We did that one year too."

So, I flew as close to the Never bird as I dared and shouted, "Boo!"

The Never bird cocked its head toward me and stared at me with one black beady eye, clucking in a disapproving way. If it could talk, I'm sure that it would've said, *You didn't really think that would work, did you?*

"No, like this." Prank burst through the leaves, just a couple feet from the Never bird, yelling and waving his arms. With a squawk, the bird launched itself into the air toward him, but as soon as Prank retreated, it sailed right back to its nest and settled back over its eggs possessively.

Prank scratched his head sheepishly. "I guess they still remember us trying that before."

"Why don't we just tap it on the shoulder and see if it'll give us a ride somewhere?" I said.

I meant it as a joke, but Kyle said, "Good idea."

He flew up really close to the Never bird we couldn't scare.

Then, grinning, he jumped on the Never bird's back. The bird didn't like it one bit. It squawked and screeched furiously while Kyle clung to its neck like a cowboy at a rodeo.

I'll tell you one thing: Kyle was pretty gutsy. The bird *was* bigger than he was.

"Now, why didn't I think of that?" Prank said, sounding faintly jealous as the bird flew jerkily, trying to knock the littlest Lost Boy off its back.

"The nest! The nest!" Kyle's voice was muffled against the feathers.

I took one side of the nest, and Prank took the other. We flew it to the neighboring tree, and just as we settled it safely on a new branch, the bird finally succeeded in bucking Kyle off. At first, the Never bird didn't seem happy to find its nest in the new location. Then it landed over the eggs, folding its wings prissily, as if to tell us that *this* was the tree it really wanted to be in the whole time.

"That worked well," I said, pleased.

"That was *awesome!*" said Kyle, still laughing. He had feathers in his hair.

"My turn!" Dibs cried, leaping from the grass and zooming into the Tree Home toward the next nest. Button followed close behind. Peter zipped up beside me and grinned, the feather on Hook's hat blowing in the breeze.

It didn't surprise me much that everyone wanted to help with the Never birds now that it wasn't boring.

What surprised me was that suddenly, *I* was the only one who had to take charge. Being naturally bossy turned out to be kind of helpful.

"Wait, let's do this right and have a real contest," Prank said as I flew around the Tree Home, counting nests. "One at a time. I'll go last." Peter gave him a look, and Prank added hastily, "I mean, second to last. Peter goes last, of course."

"Okay, there are twenty-one nests," I said, expecting the Lost Boys to rally to attention.

That definitely didn't happen.

"Me first!" Dibs cried, zooming toward the closest Never bird.

"Wait a sec!" I cried. "Button, help me with the nest."

Button looked disappointed, but he came with me anyway. Dibs pounced on the Never bird, holding on behind the wings instead of around the neck. As soon as the bird started flying, Button and I grabbed the nest, and Peter and the Lost Boys started chanting, "One, two, three . . ."

We settled the nest quickly on the other tree. You could actually hear the bird pecking Dibs. Mainly because he shouted, "Ouchies! *Ouchies!*"

At the count of fifteen, Dibs let go, sliding off the bird's back and rubbing the peck marks on his arms.

"My turn!" Button said, rushing forward, which

meant that I had to grab Kyle to help me with the next nest.

It was like that the *whole* time. Mom would've been proud of how responsible I was.

I moved every single nest, but I had to keep recruiting a new Lost Boy to help me every time I did it. Like Button, they kept getting distracted by the contest and leaving as soon as we relocated a nest.

Dibs always held his arms in the wrong place. The Never birds could peck him, and he could only stand so many pecks before letting go. Button had it tough too. The Never birds couldn't carry his weight when he was on their back. Bird and boy plummeted immediately, and Button had to keep jumping off before they struck the ground. Kyle was probably the best among the Lost Boys. He was so little that the Never birds took a little while to notice what was on their backs.

Even though the contest had been his idea, Prank didn't get a chance to try at all. Every time he got close, the Never bird flew into a rage, squawking and nipping at his outstretched hands.

"I think they remember you, Prank," Dibs said, laughing.

"They couldn't," Prank said, peeking out from the branch he was hiding behind to make sure it was safe. "I haven't collected tail feathers in *ages*."

"He used to pluck them out," Button explained to me.

I snorted. "Well, wouldn't *you* remember if someone yanked out chunks of your hair?"

Only one Never bird gave us *real* trouble, though. It happened about halfway through the contest.

Kyle landed on her back and got her out of the tree just fine, but when Button and I tried to move the nest, it wouldn't budge. It was way too heavy.

"Why does it weigh so much more than the others?" I asked Button, staring at the nest.

Without a word, Button pointed at the eggs—or rather the stones. They were smooth river rocks, the same size and shape as the other Never birds' eggs, but they were definitely *not* eggs.

Outside the tree, the Never bird twisted in midair, and Kyle fell off.

The bird landed in her nest and nipped at Button and me, forcing us back. She crouched over her stones protectively and squawked at us, just like they were real eggs.

It made me feel a little sorry for her. "You do know that they won't hatch, right?" I said gently.

The Never bird sat down on top of her nest, spreading her wings carefully, and then she stared at me and Button defiantly. Her feathers were the same dappled color as the gray bark under her, but she had a black dot on her beak, which made it a lot easier to see her.

"I think she knows," Button said. "See how she's littler than the other Never birds? Maybe she's too young to lay eggs. She must be Pretending."

"Is that right, Spot? Do you mind if I call you Spot?" I asked, pointing to the mark on her beak. She didn't squawk angrily or anything, so I guessed that meant she didn't mind. "Are you Pretending?"

Spot tilted her head at me and settled herself more comfortably over her egg-stones. I decided that meant yes.

It wasn't *that* hard to believe. Plenty of kids played house. Why couldn't a young Never bird play nest?

"We know how to handle those," Prank said wickedly, flying up and drawing one leg back.

Spot squawked furiously, and when I realized that Prank was planning to kick the nest out of the tree, I cried, "No! The eggs!"

Prank gave me a look. "But why? They're not *real*."

Button stared too, and even Spot clucked questioningly.

It just didn't seem right. *I* would hate it if I'd been playing make-believe and someone bigger and stronger than me messed it up.

"We're going to move it—all of us," I said decisively. "Dibs, you too." To the Never bird, I added, "Spot, would you mind moving for a sec? Otherwise, it might still be too heavy for us, and we might drop it."

Spot looked at me, and then at the Lost Boys, and then at her egg-stones, clucking over them uncertainly. For a second, I was afraid that she wouldn't move, but then she took flight, gliding over to the other tree.

It took all five of us to move the nest—with a little help from Pan. When one of the egg-stones fell out, Peter caught it. But we got the nest moved. When we settled it on the branch, the Lost Boys flew off to continue their contest, but when Spot landed, she rubbed her head against my hand. She was the only Never bird to acknowledge us after we moved a nest—let alone act grateful.

Peter won the contest, of course. As soon as he hopped onto one of the Never birds, it glided off the branch, tame under his hands. It happened on all three of his turns.

"That's not *fair*," Prank mumbled, watching Peter fly calmly around the clearing on the back of a Never bird yet again. He rubbed the side of his head, which he had knocked against a thick branch a few attempts earlier.

"All the Never birds like Peter," Dibs said.

"He saved one of their nests once, a long time ago," Button explained.

"Then they should really like *me*." I was sweating,

and my pajama shirt was covered in enough feathers to fill a pillow. We had already relocated almost twenty nests. "Since I kept Prank from kicking all the nests out of the tree."

"I bet my way was better," Prank said defensively. "I don't see you risking your neck and jumping on any Never birds."

"She's a *girl*," Dibs said as we settled the nest on a new branch. "Girls are scared of Never birds."

They *definitely* had old-fashioned ideas about girls. Very *annoying* ones.

"I am *not*," I said, hands on my hips. First, they called me stupid. Then they called me a coward. I wasn't going to put up with *that* any longer. "I would've done it right after Kyle, but I've been too busy carrying nests back and forth. Unlike *some* people."

"The Wendy girl should try," Peter said, looking at me as he glided by on the Never bird's back. I was especially annoyed that he was so bossy. I didn't see *him* covered in feathers.

"Fine," I said, flying up.

I almost lost my nerve when the Never bird looked straight at me, very suspicious.

"Remember what Prank wanted to do to your nests," I told it sternly, and I jumped. The Never bird took flight immediately, and I clung to its neck, waiting for it to start pecking. The feathers were so plush across its back that it felt like a warm pillow. When the wings beat and brushed my legs, they tickled my feet.

"The Never birds like her, too!" Kyle cried, delighted. "Do they always like the Wendy girls?"

I looked up, realizing that the bird wasn't going to try to knock me off.

"No," Prank told Kyle in a quiet, slightly awed voice.

The Lost Boys watched, gaping; and seeing the jealousy in Dibs's face, I felt a surge of triumph. "Don't forget the nest," I pointed out smugly, and Button and Kyle rushed to get it.

"That's just one bird," Prank said, crossing his arms. "Let's see you do it again."

So, as soon as Button and Kyle settled the nest in the other tree, I flew over the second-to-last nest in the tree. The Never bird squawked uncertainly as I climbed onto its back, but other than that, it flew out of the Tree Home without a protest while the Lost Boys moved its nest.

Before Prank could say anything else, I flew back and leaped onto the last Never bird. It sighed deeply through its beak and took flight, sailing around the clearing.

"Three!" Kyle cried, a little out of breath from transporting so many nests one after the other. "That's just as many as Peter."

"Yeah," said Prank reluctantly. "Our new Wendy

girl has a talent for Never birds."

Feeling incredibly pleased with myself, I scratched the Never bird's head. It trilled happily as we lapped the clearing a second time.

Then I saw Peter. His expression was stony.

I remembered how he had acted when I did more cartwheels than he did, back among the stars.

Too late, it occurred to me that he might have liked being the only one who could tame a Never bird. Nobody likes being shown up, especially by a visitor.

"Well," I said as modestly as I could, "I learn from the best."

8
The Never Trees Attack Pirates

*R*ight after that, Prank started complaining that his stomach was growling, and when Button pointed out that they had missed lunch, Peter and Tink flew off to find us something to eat.

He gave me a weird look as he went. If I didn't know any better, I would say that he was looking at me like I'd just shown up in the clearing—like he was seeing me for the first time. But all he said was "Lost Boys, make sure the Wendy girl doesn't try to befriend any mermaids while I'm gone."

Most of the Lost Boys laughed like Peter had told them to stop me from making friends with Neverland's crocodile or something equally outrageous.

Only Button turned to me curiously. "You tried to make friends with the mermaids?"

I shrugged, flushing a little and wishing Peter hadn't brought it up. I had enough trouble winning the Lost Boys over without Peter making me seem idiotic.

"Wendy girl, we can take a break until after dinner, right?" Kyle asked after Peter left. His shoulders drooped, like he was really tired. "I'm starving."

"Okay," I said, more than happy to rest. Remembering how I'd almost dropped Dad's camera earlier, I asked, "Is there a safe place I can hide my camera for the night? I don't want to mess it up."

"There's the hiding places," Button suggested as he joined the others.

"You can put it in mine!" Kyle said, flying down a few branches. Then he grasped a knob in the trunk firmly, twisted, and pulled. A big chunk of bark swung on hinges, revealing a locker space behind it.

"Wow," I said, passing the camera to Kyle. It was a bit shadowy inside the hiding place, and hard to see, but a very worn teddy bear peeked out.

Kyle placed my dad's camera inside with exaggerated care. "We all have one. Button made them."

I was starting to realize that Button made almost everything around the Tree Home.

But I didn't realize how tired I was until I sat down with the Lost Boys among the lower branches. Or maybe I was just *really* ready for dinner. I hadn't eaten *anything* since pizza the night before.

My stomach growled, so loudly that all the Lost Boys turned to stare.

"I'm hungry too," said Kyle with a huge sigh. "Too bad this isn't a food tree."

I glanced at the branch above us, looking for apples or oranges or lemons I might have missed among the leaves. "I don't see any fruit."

"A *food tree*," said Dibs, as if it were the most obvious thing in the world. Suddenly, he reminded me a *lot* of Peter. "Don't you know the difference?"

"Of course she doesn't," Kyle said, scowling at Dibs. "Neverland is the only place that has food trees."

"We have fruit trees," I said, thinking that they just weren't saying the name right. "Is that what you mean?"

"No," said Button, Prank, Kyle, and Dibs together.

"Food trees are special," said Button. "Neverland didn't always have them, but once, a Wendy girl brought a *huge* basket of food to Neverland to share with us Lost Boys. We had a picnic."

"After we finished eating, there was a lot left over. We started a food fight. It was my idea," Prank added proudly.

"The Wendy girl got mad—like a real mother would," Dibs said. "She lectured us. She said, 'Your mother has worked hard to prepare that meal for you. Food doesn't grow on trees, you know.'"

I wrinkled my nose. I'd heard *that* before. Grandma Delaney said it all the time. Was she the Wendy girl they meant?

"But Peter said, 'Says who?'" Kyle added excitedly.

"How do you know? You weren't there," Dibs said.

"I've heard the story."

"Then Peter scooped up handfuls of crumbs from the food fight, dug holes all around, and planted the crumbs like seeds," said Button. "After he covered the crumbs with dirt and watered them, he Pretended with all his might."

"The next day, the clearing where we'd eaten the picnic had become a grove of food trees," said Prank.

"Can Peter do that?" I said, surprised.

"He's Peter *Pan*," Dibs said, scoffingly. "He can do anything."

"I don't know if the Pretending would've worked anywhere else, though," Button said with a thoughtful frown. "It's part of Neverland's magic."

"Does that mean that Spot's stone eggs will hatch?" I asked.

"I don't know," said Button.

"Doubt it," Prank said. "It takes a strong imagination to Pretend *that* well."

"Like Peter's," said Dibs, very proudly.

"Anyway, the grove has a bunch of different food trees," said Kyle.

"But the trees all bloom at different times," Button explained. "If we find one ready to eat, we tell Tiger Lily and her braves what it is, and they do the same for us. Tiger Lily actually came by today to tell us that the cheeseburger tree is almost ripe."

At the word *cheeseburger*, my stomach growled again. I groaned. "Can we not talk about food for a little while? Please?"

Peter came back with dinner at sunset—an armful of huge roast beef sandwiches, wrapped in brown paper. I didn't realize that food trees grew stuff like that, but since the Lost Boys didn't say anything, I figured it was normal.

We ate silently and enthusiastically. The feather on Hook's hat kept falling into Peter's face until he finally lost patience and dropped the hat onto Dibs's head. Dibs looked absolutely delighted.

We sat among the highest branches of the Tree Home. From the next tree over, the relocated Never birds watched us. It actually made me a little nervous. Like they were planning to reconquer the Tree Home or something.

Spot clucked nervously. It was a warning. Peter stood up, a hand on his golden sword, listening intently, and the Lost Boys and I craned our necks toward the ground.

We heard the pirates complaining before we saw them.

"I'm so hungry," moaned one.

"I can't go on," replied a second. "I see them little black spots, dancing in front of me eyes."

"We'll find supper when we find Peter Pan," said someone else cheerfully.

Button recognized that third voice and whispered, "It's Smee."

"Cook says Pan's nicked it," Smee continued.

In the tree, we all turned to look at Peter. He smiled mysteriously and took another enormous bite out of his dinner.

"It were my favorite," said the second voice sadly. "Roast beef sandwiches."

"Not sure if I believe Cook," the first voice grumbled. "Seems to me Cook might have taken them for his*self* and blamed Pan."

We could see them now. The pirates had wandered into the clearing below, just fifty feet from the trunk of our tree.

"Oh, it was Pan all right," Smee said. He was a little thicker around the middle than the other two. With his glasses, white hair, and red nose, he looked a little bit like Santa Claus's pirate brother. "I heard him crow with me own ears, I did."

"Look!" I whispered, pointing at the tallest pirate. "Are his hands on backward?"

Button nodded solemnly. "That's Noodler."

"The other one looks like Black Patch Pat," added Dibs.

"They'll be sorry they came here," Peter said in a low voice, drawing his weapon.

It must've been a signal. Even Tink chimed a little softer. The Lost Boys moved quickly and silently to hiding places like Kyle's in the trunk, where they pulled out swords of their own.

I felt a little left out. I didn't have a sword yet.

"What do we have here?" Smee had found the blankets on the ground. He held up a particularly rumpled blue one, and the other two pirates came over to inspect it. "Someone's been sleeping in this bed, I think. We must be getting closer. The cap'n will be *so* happy when we bring back his hat."

"Now we really will have to move again," Kyle murmured to Button.

Move? After all the nests we'd relocated? *I* didn't want to have done all that work for nothing, and I definitely didn't want to end up sleeping on the ground somewhere while pirates roamed the forest.

"What if we *don't* go out there?" I asked suddenly.

This was the wrong thing to say. Thinking I was

scared, the Lost Boys all turned to me with scornful looks.

"Don't worry, Wendy girl. *You* don't need to do anything," Peter said, suddenly very superior and smug. He swung his sword magnificently. "We'll protect you."

I glared at him. If *he* was going to fight, I wasn't going to hide in the tree, but that wasn't what I'd meant. "No, what if we did something *else*? Something where they never saw us?"

"Like a trick?" Prank asked, suddenly interested.

I nodded, and Prank turned to Peter with a bright, begging look.

"Smee! There's something here!" Black Patch Pat had stumbled upon the photos the Lost Boys had left in a pile on the grass. The pirate picked up one and squinted at it in the dusky light. "It looks like Pan, sir, but very small."

The rest of the Lost Boys watched Peter with that same hopeful look.

"We can make it seem like Neverland itself is defending you," I whispered to Peter, "but we have to act fast."

Peter glanced at all the Lost Boys and nodded deeply.

I whispered my plan. Prank caught on first and began climbing down to the lowest branches.

All three pirates had gathered around the Polaroids.

Smee took the photo from Black Patch Pat carefully. "It does certainly look like Pan," he said after inspecting it through his glasses. "How did he get in this little flat square?"

"Something the fairies cooked up?" Noodler suggested. "One of their pixie-brained plots?"

Tink hissed, outraged, and Peter hushed her.

"Has Pan been imprisoned at last?" Smee said.

Then it was up to me to keep Peter from going out and defending his reputation. "The great Pan is never caught," he said, not quietly enough.

I held on tight to his sword arm and whispered, "Just think how you'll trick them—how you've already tricked them."

That was when the attack started. Prank pulled a branch so far back that when he let go, it whistled through the air and smacked into Noodler's side. Noodler jumped and looked around wildly as the Lost Boys spread out among the lower branches right above the pirates.

Smee and Black Patch Pat didn't look away from the photos. "If he's imprisoned, then why is he smiling?" asked Black Patch Pat. "Here's another little Pan!" he added, picking up a second photograph.

Prank found another branch, a larger one, and aimed at Noodler again. The poor pirate yelped when it struck him.

"Quiet, Noodler," Smee said absently. To Black Patch Pat, he said, "We'll have to show 'em to the cap'n."

"Something's been hitting me!" Noodler said, starting to sound mad.

At this point, all of the Lost Boys had gotten the hang of it. They each let go of a branch at the same time, pummeling the pirates. Smee got leaves in his beard, and Black Patch Pat started saying words that Mom once grounded me for repeating.

"It's the trees!" cried Noodler, drawing his sword. "They've come alive."

The Lost Boys could barely keep themselves from laughing. Kyle started snorting softly through his nose.

"Such a thing has never happened in Neverland before," Smee said. His voice wobbled with fear. He pushed up his spectacles to examine the tree, but he couldn't see the Lost Boys. The light was too dim, the leaves on the lower branches too thick. "We must tell the cap'n."

Tink flew down and started her own barrage, slapping them with light branches so fast that they looked like an endless blur of green.

"To your weapons! To your weapons!" cried Smee, sounding really scared now. "Fight the tree to the death!"

My plan was working! While the Lost Boys distracted

the pirates, Peter and I zipped up to the top branches, and then over to the tree next door, where the relocated Never birds still sat in their nests.

"Go out there," Peter told the closest one. "All of you. Chase them away."

The Never birds glared at him, as if he had gone crazy. Peter's eyebrows rose really high. He'd expected them to follow his orders immediately.

Below us, Black Patch Pat wailed. "My eye! My one good eye!"

"*Now,*" Peter said in his angriest, most commanding tone.

I tried a different approach. Looking straight at Spot, I said, "They're a threat to your nests."

"Oww!!!" shouted all three pirates at once. Tink had pulled back another branch, one so big that it knocked the pirates to the ground. Fairies must be really strong for their size.

Inspired by her success, the Lost Boys started to team up so that they could pull back bigger branches too.

"Do you know what they'll do if they find your eggs?" I told the Never birds, who watched *me* now instead of Peter. "They'll *eat* them."

That got the Never birds' attention. Several clucked in a threatening way. Spot's feathers started to ruffle.

I dropped my voice to a whisper, like I was telling a secret. "I thought you should know—I heard them talking about Never bird *omelets*."

That did it. The Never birds burst out of the tree, squawking and furious. They swooped down at the pirates and pecked at their heads. Spot even tore a chunk out of Smee's hat.

Noodler and Black Patch Pat both screamed, throwing up their arms to protect their faces. "Retreat!" Smee shouted, and the pirates ran out of the clearing and into the forest.

Peter crowed in triumph. The Lost Boys cheered too, and even Tink twinkled in a pleased way.

"Thank you, Never birds," I said, feeling very smug as the flock flapped back to their nests. If this didn't prove I wasn't the stupidest visitor they'd ever had, then nothing would. "That went well, I think."

"I like this Wendy girl," Kyle told Peter as I flew down to the blankets and Polaroids.

"She's very clever. That's why I brought her," Peter said, and I smiled wider.

Half buried under the blankets, I found what I had been hoping for—a sword, straight and silver, that came to a nice sharp point. One of the pirates had left it behind.

I admired the pretty swirling guard around the hilt and wondered when I would get a chance to use it.

9 I Find Out
I'm Good at Pretending

*K*yle jabbed again with his short, flat blade. I scrambled out of the way, but not quickly enough. The point of Kyle's sword caught my pajamas, and the fabric ripped.

The littlest Lost Boy lowered his weapon. "Oops. Sorry, Wendy girl."

I looked down at my pajamas and sighed. Kyle had torn a palm-sized hole in the knee.

The Lost Boys had been trying to teach me how to use my new sword. It wasn't going all that well.

Peter lay back lazily in midair, as if an invisible lounge chair hung in the sky, and he played his pipes, watching us. I had the feeling he still didn't know what to do with me, but after tricking the pirates, we'd gotten past the taking-me-home-early idea.

While I practiced, the moon had risen, brightening everyone's blades with its silvery light. Unfortunately, I had gotten a little sweaty and *a lot* frustrated, but not any better.

"You're in trouble now, Kyle," Dibs said, smirking a little from his perch in the lower branches of the Tree Home. "Wendy girls are very particular about their clothes."

I wasn't upset about that. I was upset that my sword and I weren't getting along, but Kyle's eyes still got really big.

"It's okay," I told him. "Neverland is a little too hot for long pants anyway." I grabbed a handful of loose fabric and tugged, ripping straight across until the bottom of the torn pajama leg came completely off.

The Lost Boys stared at me like no Wendy girl in the history of Neverland had ever ripped her clothes on purpose. Dibs's mouth even gaped open.

"They're just pajamas," I pointed out, trying not to laugh.

"You should probably do the other side," Button said solemnly.

I nodded. "Kyle, if you could," I said, gesturing to the other pajama leg, and with a giggle, Kyle used his sword to make a tear near that knee. I grabbed the hem and ripped the bottom of the leg right off. Suddenly, I had shorts instead of pants. "At home, we call these cutoffs."

A gentle Neverland breeze swirled around my ankles, and I felt much, *much* cooler.

"Now you look like one of us," Prank said. His pants had holes in them, and his shirt was stained with mud and grass. But he smiled like it was a compliment, so I grinned back.

"Yeah, but you need to fight like us too," Dibs said. "Otherwise, Peter won't let you go on adventures. Right, Peter?"

We all looked up at Peter. He nodded, moving his pipes along with his head so that he didn't have to stop playing.

"Again," I said to Kyle, raising my sword.

Kyle swung his sword. I blocked it, just barely, but then Kyle hooked his hilt around mine. My new sword fell to the ground with a clatter.

The fairy chimed in a smug way, and Dibs grinned. "Tink's right. You *are* hopeless."

"I am *not*," I said, snatching the sword back and glaring at Dibs. I was too embarrassed to look at Peter.

Sighing deeply, Kyle raised his weapon high above his head, and I watched him, trying to guess where he would strike and how I could counter it.

"Wendy girl, you're thinking too hard," Button said suddenly.

"No, I'm not," I said, feeling even more defensive. "I just need a little more practice, that's all."

"Oooooh," said the Lost Boys together, as if a great mystery had been revealed.

"That's your problem, then," said Kyle sympathetically, lowering his sword. "I had the same trouble when I first came to Neverland."

"You don't need to *practice*," said Prank. "You need to Pretend."

"You know the saying *Practice makes perfect*? It doesn't work here," said Button. "In Neverland, it's *Pretend* that makes perfect."

All four of them—even Dibs—looked at me earnestly, waiting for me to do something, and I stared back, confused. "Wait. *What* am I supposed to do?"

"You have to Pretend to be a great swordsman," said Dibs, rolling his eyes.

"Swords*woman*," I said automatically, but I still didn't understand.

"Look—at home, you would've had to practice and practice and practice to get good," said Kyle, "but you're in Neverland now. In Neverland, Pretending is even better than being something for real. If you Pretend that you're already a great swordswoman, you will be one, and then no pirate will ever stand a chance against our Wendy girl."

I nodded slowly. I could do that. Michael and I pretended to be sailors and explorers and stuff in the tree house at home all the time.

It just *had* to work—if it didn't, I would get stuck watching from the sidelines the next time Peter and the Lost Boys fought a battle.

I stared at my sword and Pretended as hard as I could: I was Ashley Delaney, famed swordswoman, Wendy girl as no Wendy girl had ever been, feared by pirates for her strength and cunning and skill. My blade had defeated many a foe already, and word had spread to the far reaches of Neverland.

My toes and fingers tingled again, just like they had that morning when Peter and I had flown toward the island. But it was stronger. It felt more like it does when your foot falls asleep and then starts to wake up.

Suddenly, the sword felt more comfortable in my hand, like I had been using it all my life. Instead of feeling sore at the exertion, the muscles in my arm kind of liked the weight of the sword. It was almost reassuring.

To test it out, I tried a little flourish.

"Oh, good," said Kyle. "That's much better."

I looked at the Lost Boys, and through my Pretending, I knew without a shadow of a doubt that I could fight them and win.

Grinning, I told them, "Again—all four of you this time!"

Without any hesitation, Kyle, Prank, Button, and

Dibs all leaped toward me, swords raised. I sprang up into the air to meet them.

I blocked Kyle's sword so hard that the force sent him spinning back through the trees, head over feet, giggling and trailing fairy dust.

Prank tried to catch my blade between both of his, but I twisted my weapon so his two swords went flying.

Dibs stabbed toward me, and I turned the blow aside, straight into the tree trunk behind me. The point of Dibs's sword slid into the wood and stuck fast.

And Button—poor Button—was so surprised that he dropped his sword and raised both hands in surrender.

"Hurrah for the Wendy girl!" Kyle said, flying back into the clearing with twigs tangled in his hair. "I *knew* you would be good at Pretending."

Peter blew a triumphant little ditty into his pipes, grinning at me, and then flew high above the trees and out of sight. But we could still hear him crow.

I was so happy with my success that I rose into the air, and took a quick bow about a foot off the ground. Prank, Kyle, and Button applauded.

"Thanks," I said, dropping to the grass and picking up Button's sword. When I handed it back, he took it from me sheepishly.

"But why did you have to be better than all of us?" Dibs said grumpily, trying to wiggle his blade out of the wood. I scowled at him.

"It just means that she can Pretend better than the rest of us," Button said in his quiet way.

"Exactly what we should expect from our newest Wendy girl," said Prank proudly, and I beamed, glad I was beginning to win them over.

Dibs snorted, clearly not satisfied. With one last tug, he freed his sword from the tree trunk, taking a huge chunk of wood with it. "Good at Pretending to be everything but our mother, you mean."

I threw him a dirty look. He had no reason to bring *that* up again except to make me look bad, but then the other Lost Boys descended to the ground slowly, hanging their heads as if a very sad thought had come over all of them. That's the trouble with fairy dust— people can tell exactly what you're feeling just by looking at you.

It was really hard not to feel guilty.

I remembered the little imitation of Mom I had done earlier that day—with the twig glasses and bark paper. Someone had mentioned Pretending then. The Lost Boys probably thought I had been using Neverland's magic rather than just faking.

Now that I knew better, I probably should've Pretended to be a mom—just to see whether or not I could.

But I didn't.

I didn't want the Lost Boys to like me just because I Pretended to be their mother. Maybe I would make some cookies, but if they got me patching their clothes and tucking them in at night, they wouldn't think of me as a friend. I wanted them to like me for me.

They still didn't realize that a Wendy girl could have a few good adventures up her sleeve. At least, not *yet*.

"I'm sorry," I told the Lost Boys, and I meant it.

Button must've heard how sincere I was. "It's okay."

"It's *not* okay," said Dibs, returning his sword to his hiding spot and slamming the door shut. I squirmed uncomfortably.

"Wendy girl, if you can't be our mother, then could you maybe tell us a *story* about mothers?" asked Kyle, and all the Lost Boys looked at me eagerly, rising a little and hovering a few inches above the ground.

"A story? About Mom?" I repeated, a little panicky. Mom breaking her promise about the Christmas tree probably wasn't the kind of story that the Lost Boys wanted, but that was the first one that came to mind.

"Yeah!" said Kyle enthusiastically.

"You have a mother, right?" said Dibs with a touch of mockery.

"Tell us something about her," said Prank, just as excited as Kyle.

"Like what did she do when you last saw her?" asked Button.

"She . . ." My mind scrambled backward through my memories. For a minute, yesterday seemed very far away—adventures and adventures ago. Then I remembered watching the twin red lights on my parents' car as they disappeared down the street. All the hurt and disappointment came rushing back, as fresh as ever.

"She *left*," I said shortly, and my voice caught on the second word.

"*Oh*," said all the Lost Boys at once, coming back to the ground with a thud, and sympathy shone on all their faces. Even Dibs's, although he didn't say anything. He just climbed up into the Tree Home and disappeared among the higher branches.

"We understand," said Button. "We've *all* lost our mothers somehow."

"Usually, though, Lost Boys just get—you know—lost. I've never heard of a mother *leaving*," said Prank. "No wonder you came to Neverland."

"You're better off here," said Kyle, patting my shoulder with a comforting smile. "Maybe you'll stay and become a Lost Girl."

I didn't know what to say. I hadn't *planned* to stay forever. Could I? Mom and Dad were probably home. By Tuesday, they'd be done with their work, and then it would be Christmas.

But it was nice to feel accepted. So, I didn't say anything.

"Neverland doesn't have any Lost Girls." Prank frowned at Kyle.

"So?" said Kyle. "I bet once it didn't have any Lost Boys either. She could be the *first* Lost Girl."

"Impossible. Do you think that will strike fear into Hook's heart?" To me, Prank added, "It's not personal, but we do have to protect our reputation. I can just hear Smee now: 'Look, Cap'n—here come Peter Pan, the Lost Boys, and a Lost Girl.' It totally messes up the sound of it."

Prank did a really good impression of Smee—the same raspy accent and the overexaggerated cheerfulness. I couldn't help giggling.

Button wasn't paying attention. He was examining the tree. "We should probably get your bed set up, before it gets any later."

10
Button Makes Me a Hammock

*B*ed. Just hearing the word made me realize how tired I was, even more tired than I'd been earlier. My arms were sluggish with weariness, my eyelids heavy. Apparently, sleeping on the back of the wind hadn't given me the most restful night ever. "Okay," I said. "Tell me what I need to do."

"We make the hammocks out of two leaves," Button said. "They need to be about six feet long and right on top of each other."

I stared up at the enormous tree. Moonlight reflected off the glossy leaves. Right above us, there was a cluster of leaves no longer than my pinky finger, and a little higher to the right, a whole branch with leaves the length of my leg. I didn't see even one six-foot-long leaf.

It might be a long time before I got to sleep.

"They're usually up where the other hammock beds are," Button said, a little anxiously. "Is that okay?"

I nodded, so grateful that I had to resist the urge to hug him. Button smiled, like he was pleased to be helpful, and when he took off, I flew up after him, leaving Kyle and Prank bickering behind us.

"Maybe we could rename ourselves. We could be the Lost Children. Or the Lost Kids," said Kyle.

"The 'Lost Kids'? That still sounds stupid. If we're going to change our name, it'll have to be just as cool as what we already have."

Button flew to the row of branches directly below Peter's red house, maybe seventy-five feet above the ground. There, the four leaf hammocks Prank had shown me earlier swayed a little in the breeze. One of them was occupied.

"Good night, Dibs," Button called, but Dibs just scowled at us both and drew a ragged blanket up until it covered his face.

"Don't mind him," Button whispered, landing on a branch a little above the other hammocks, directly opposite Peter's house. "Dibs just really wanted a mother."

Even with the blanket, you could still see how upset he was—something about how his body was all hunched up. It made me want to apologize again, but I didn't know how. Especially since I had this feeling that Dibs would just say something nasty like he had before.

Button tugged two leaves of the right size into place until they were matched from end to end above and below the branch they grew from. One leaf's waxy side faced the sky, and the other faced the ground.

"What's the top leaf for?" I asked.

"To keep the rain off." Button held the stems tightly to the top and bottom of the branch with both hands. "Can you hold it in place—just like this?"

I placed my hands exactly like Button had. Each stem was as thick around as my big toe. "It rains in Neverland?"

"Thunderstorms, mostly," Button said, inspecting the tree's trunk, where a number of vines snaked up toward the sky. He tested each of them and then picked a thick one, grabbing the end and pulling it off. "You know, Dibs won't say it, and neither will the others, but we're really glad that you saved us from having to move."

"I did?" I asked, surprised.

"Yeah—when you stopped Peter from chasing away the pirates." Button began to wrap the vine around the stems I was holding down. "Whenever Peter attacks from a tree, Hook figures that he must live there and sends his pirates to investigate. We've lost our last three trees that way."

"Oh." It hadn't occurred to me that the Lost Boys wouldn't want to move either.

Button tied the vine around the branch and bound stems with an expert knot, and, tugging yards and yards of extra vine from the tree trunk, he nodded at the other side of the leaf. "Can you hold that end the same way, please?"

I flew down the branch, and, grabbing the ends of the leaf, I clamped my hands over them like Button had done on the other side. "Like this?"

"Perfect," Button said. He began to fly around and around the branch with another vine—this one more slender—weaving a net around the leaf hammock as he went. His hands were so sure and quick that I had a hard time following them in the moonlight.

It was strange to watch Button. Earlier that day, I'd thought that he was the most bumbling of the Lost Boys, but as he wrapped the last of the vine around the ends of the leaves I held down, Button seemed as confident as Peter.

"Cool," I said. The netting looked pretty professional.

Tying the final knot, Button ducked his head

bashfully. "Well, I may not be a very good fighter, but I can always make things. Would you mind testing it out?"

I wiggled through one of the larger holes in the netting and lay down carefully on the bottom leaf, staring at the branch above me. I was ready to fly up again if the hammock showed any sign of falling, but the net around the bottom leaf held my weight without even creaking. The inside had a soft texture, a little bit like flannel. That leaf hammock was actually more comfortable than my bed at home.

I almost fell asleep right then, but Button asked, a little anxiously, "Well? Is it okay?"

"Wow," I said, sitting up abruptly and fighting my way awake again. "You're really *good* at making things."

Button ducked his head, not wanting to show how proud he felt. "Want to see something else I made?"

I kind of wanted to get straight to sleep, but I didn't want to offend him when he was being so nice to me. "Sure," I said, flying quickly out of bed before I drifted off again.

Button flew down to the branch below us, one that was right next to a leaf hammock (it was so much wider than the others that I suspected that it was his). A few leaves as long as my arm leaned up against the trunk, and when he removed them,

Button looked at me eagerly.

There, carved straight into the trunk, was a ship sailing on a choppy sea. *Captain Hook's pirate ship*, I realized, flying closer and squinting in the dim light. A flag with a skull and crossbones hung from the mast, and the words *Jolly Roger* had been added on the hull. The ship was so wonderfully carved that the wide sails seemed to billow and ripple above the deck.

"Button, you're an *artist*," I said, astonished.

"You think so?" He stood up a little straighter, his chest swelling with pride. "I do my best. My mother was an artist. Or at least I think she was. I remember her standing in front of an easel with a paintbrush. It's actually *all* that I can remember." His voice wobbled; but when I looked up in alarm, wondering if he was all right, his face was blank, without a trace of sadness.

He obviously didn't want anyone to know that he missed his mother, so I pretended not to notice, concentrating on the tree trunk.

A little farther down, I spotted another carving—a lion, every hair in his mane crafted separately, his jaws opened in a roar. Each tooth looked sharp enough to pierce the skin. "I love this one. I can almost hear him."

Button ducked his head bashfully again, but it had to have been a happy thought. He rose at least three feet in the air. "There's the one I'm carving now," he said, pointing to a charcoal sketch a little below the lion—a humanlike figure with short hair, wings, and a rose-petal dress. So far, only one foot had been carved.

I knew exactly who it was supposed to be. "Tinker Bell."

"Don't tell her it's here. Otherwise, she'll sneak up all the time to see how much I've carved."

I nodded, smirking. If Tink reacted to this carving the same way that she had to the Polaroid earlier, she would become a *major* pain in the butt.

Farther down, I saw drawings of leaves and lions and fairies and something that looked a lot like Peter's house, circling around the trunk and out of sight. "But why would you carve it all the way up here? If you made it closer to the ground, more people could admire your work. You definitely deserve to be admired."

At the compliment, Button rose even higher with a proud smile. "I just wanted to decorate the staircase a little."

"The staircase?" Then, for the first time, I noticed the steps that wound around the tree. They blended in almost as much as a Never bird, because each step rested either on the base of a branch or on an extra-large knot protruding from the trunk. I might not have seen the staircase at all, but each step had a groove in the middle, as if many feet had worn a path.

"Whoa—where did that come from?"

"Well, we Pretended it there. The Lost Boys, I mean. A while ago. It took all four of us concentrating really hard," said Button. "Peter and Tink had been off on an adventure for so long that we ran out of fairy dust. We couldn't fly, so we either had to imagine ourselves a staircase to get to the hammocks or spend the night sleeping on the ground."

I looked at Button curiously. If the Lost Boys could Pretend a staircase onto their tree, what else could be Pretended into being?

11
We Fake a Thunderstorm

"You have to stay here."

"No, I don't. You need my help."

The voices woke me up, but it took me a moment to recognize them. I rubbed my eyes and stared around me in sleepy confusion. The light shining through the leaves was still weak and gray. The sun wasn't even up yet.

"I've handled it plenty of times on my own."

"Yeah, but you said yourself that this particular harvest isn't a one-Lost-Boy job."

I was sleeping between two giant leaves, inside a net woven from vines.

That's right—I was in Neverland!

I sat up, suddenly wide-awake. I refused to sleep anymore if I could have adventures instead. As soon as that occurred to me, I started to float. Excitement can do that to a Wendy girl.

"Well, it's not really a two-Lost-Boy job either, so it would be better if you stayed here. You'll only get in my way."

"I won't. Prank, I promise I won't."

I peered over the edge of the leaf hammock. Prank flew across the clearing, carrying something that I couldn't make out in the dim light. Kyle gave himself a running start and jumped up in the air, chasing after Prank.

They were going to do something way more exciting than spring cleaning. I just knew it. I wiggled through the leaf-hammock net and raced after them, following the sound of their voices.

"Go *back*, Kyle. The fairies will recognize you."

"Won't they recognize *you*? You're the one who always goes over there. Besides, you promised to let me help."

I ducked under a leafy branch and found them. Prank carried a large flat sheet of metal under his arm. It looked a lot like a cookie sheet. He also had a bucket hanging from his elbow and a plastic watering can in his other hand, but Kyle was trying to wrestle the watering can away.

"Hey, guys," I said as casually as possible.

"Good morning!" said Kyle.

"Oh, no—not you, too," said Prank with a groan.

"What are you guys up to?"

"We're going to the fairies' tree to harvest fairy dust!" Kyle cried. "That way, we'll still be able to fly even if Tink gets mad and refuses to give us any."

The fairies' tree! I would love to see more fairies.

"Except it's not 'we.' I'm the only one going," said Prank.

"Prank, that's not fair!"

"I can't have you messing things up. Tricking an entire tree of fairies is a very delicate operation."

"Well, of *course* Kyle wants to come," I said quickly, cutting in before the argument got really carried away. "Your tricks are *legendary* in Neverland. It's only natural we would want to see you in action."

"But I want to *help*—," Kyle started to protest, but I shot him a warning look. I knew what I was doing. Sometimes, a little flattery could go a long way. Well, much farther than arguing or begging anyway.

Prank's mouth twitched oddly, like he wanted to smile very wide, but he thought it might be beneath his dignity as someone legendary in Neverland. "Fine, you can come," he said finally, passing the watering can to Kyle and the oversized cookie sheet to me. "But you better do everything *exactly* how I tell you."

"Yes!" Kyle cried, and, hugging the cookie sheet to my chest, I hid a triumphant smile.

Dodging tree limbs, we flew after Prank, who still carried the bucket in the crook of his elbow. "Your goal," Prank said, sounding more serious than I'd ever heard him, "is to lure the fairies out of their tree long enough for me to collect the fairy dust."

Overcome with excitement, Kyle began to snort softly through his nose, grinning widely.

Prank stopped and gave him a stern look. "This is no laughing matter, Kyle. If you can't settle down and focus, then I really will make you go back."

Kyle clamped his hand over his mouth, and I felt for him. I definitely knew what it was like for people to threaten to send you home.

"So, what's the plan?" I asked.

Prank turned away and started flying through the trees again. "To get all the fairies out at the same time, they have to believe that something irresistible is outside. The only thing *all* fairies find *completely* irresistible is—"

"A thunderstorm!" Kyle interrupted, letting his hand fall from his mouth.

"But why?" I asked, privately thinking that his plan was a little far-fetched.

"Because a lightning bolt will grant a wish," Prank

said. "*If* they can catch it."

For the fairies' sake, I hoped that lightning bolts were less deadly in Neverland than they were at home.

The idea excited Kyle so much that he started sailing through the trees a little higher than Prank and me, giggling madly again.

"Kyle," Prank said sharply.

Kyle stopped giggling. "Sorry."

"You're Rain," Prank told him, pointing at the watering can Kyle was carrying. "Let's see you practice."

With his eyebrows pinched together and his tongue sticking out, Kyle tipped the watering can carefully. A steady shower of water spilled from the spout and plopped to the forest floor ten feet below.

"No, not like that," Prank said flatly, and Kyle's face fell. "The hard part is not to overdo it," Prank explained, a little more gently. "There's only three of us—we could probably *never* mimic a thunderstorm in full swing, *but* we can probably convince the fairies that one is starting. Kyle, you just need to sprinkle a few drops here and there."

"Maybe you can *Pretend*," I suggested, suddenly remembering what the Lost Boys had said about Pretending being better than practicing. "Just imagine that you're already a great rain faker or something."

When Kyle looked to him for permission, Prank

shrugged. "It couldn't hurt."

"Okay." Kyle concentrated again, his tongue sticking out, and he only spilled a few drops.

Prank nodded. "Much better. You're Thunder, Wendy girl."

It took me a second to remember that Prank meant me. "*Please* call me Ashley," I said as I started to Pretend, my toes and fingers tingling.

I held the cookie sheet in front of me and rattled it. It did sound a lot like thunder.

"Good. Now follow me," Prank said, flying forward.

Even though I had only seen it once before, I recognized the fairies' tree as soon as we reached it. It stood at the edge of a cliff, high above the sea. It glowed in the predawn dark, lit from the inside with hundreds of different-colored lights.

"Those are the fairies," Kyle whispered. "The white ones are girls, and the purplish ones are boys."

"What about the blue ones?" I asked.

Kyle frowned a little, thinking. "Not sure."

"Shh. No more talking," Prank said, as strict as any general before a battle. But his eyes gleamed, like he couldn't wait to get started. "We don't want to wake them up too early."

When we got close enough to see through the leaves,

I stifled a gasp. I had been impressed when I'd seen Button make the hammock the night before, but that was nothing compared to what the fairies had constructed. With a few slender vines and some big leaves folded like origami, they had created a whole town. Miniature houses sat on every branch, complete with shutters and patios. One even had a swimming pool.

A few of the larger buildings made me think that the fairies had done some traveling. I saw a castle with a moat and a drawbridge, two Eiffel Towers, a couple of pyramids with a sphinx out front, a Statue of Liberty, and a skinny structure as tall as I was, which looked a lot like the Empire State Building.

It was completely stunning. Tink had to really love Peter and the Lost Boys to decide to live with them instead of here with the other fairies. Knowing that made me wish she liked *me* more.

Spread over the ground below the tree and its leaf buildings was a layer of what looked like fine gold sugar, a few inches deep. It glowed and glittered on its own—fairy dust. Since all the fairies lived there, their dust had collected on the ground, unused and unnoticed.

With the bucket still hanging from his arm, Prank pointed upward. It was time for me and Kyle to take our places.

Okay, I know I told Prank that his tricks were

legendary, but until you saw one of his tricks in action, you really *couldn't* know how good he actually was. He had carefully plotted out every detail of mimicking a thunderstorm.

Prank stared hard at the sky, watching it lighten. He was waiting for the perfect shade of gray, the one that would look the most like cloudy sky.

Or at least, it *might*—if you were a fairy who hadn't completely woken up from a good night's sleep.

It probably would've been impossible anywhere except Neverland, but, grasping the cookie sheet firmly in both hands, I Pretended that I was the best fake-thunder maker Neverland had ever seen. My toes and fingers tingled, just like they had before. Then I flew to the top of the fairies' tree with Kyle.

Suddenly, Prank raised his arm—the signal.

Pretending as hard as I could, I rattled the cookie sheet, very gently. To my relief, it gave off a soft, echoing rumble—almost exactly like distant thunder.

With a cry like a bell, the first fairy woke.

I flew across the crown of the tree to a different part of the fairies' city and shook the cookie sheet a little harder. It sounded like the thunder had come even closer.

A dozen more fairies woke, chittering questioningly.

Prank raised his other hand. It was Kyle's turn.

The littlest Lost Boy zipped across the top of the tree

with the watering can, sprinkling a few drops here, a few drops there, just as if it were beginning to rain.

I flew around above the tree making little rumbles everywhere. Several fairies flew up out of their leaf homes and started zigzagging around the inside of their tree, chiming to the rest and waking them up. More and more fairies rose from their beds and joined the others, and the excited chittering got louder and louder. Kyle started snorting softly through his nose, grinning. He was having a really hard time keeping himself from laughing out loud. I kept one eye on Prank, waiting for the final signal.

When Prank pointed at me, I knew what I had to do.

Right above the part of the tree closest to the ocean, as my fingers and toes tingled with Pretending, I smacked the cookie sheet as hard as I could with my fist. The extra-loud thunder noise made all the fairies look in that direction. I zoomed quickly out of sight, and with a sound like a thousand bicycle bells ringing, the fairies poured out of the tree toward the water, hundreds of fist-sized lights. They searched the skies and roamed over the waves like a whirlwind of glowing sparks.

Prank didn't waste any time. As soon as the last fairy left the tree, he burst forward and flew into their leaf town, using the bucket to scoop up the abandoned fairy dust.

Kyle couldn't hold it in anymore. He burst into giggles.

A couple fairies looked back. Then, unmistakably, the swarm of fairies began to head our way.

"Run!" I cried. Tucking the cookie sheet under my arm, I raced back toward the woods, grabbing Kyle's hand on the way. Dodging branches and dragging a still-giggling Kyle, I tried not to think about what the fairies would do if they caught us. If they were anything like Tinker Bell, I didn't want to find out. For a few minutes, I could hear them following us, chattering angrily, but after we twisted deeper and deeper into the trees, they gave up the chase.

When Prank caught up with us, he glided through the air calmly, his bucket now filled to the *brim* with fairy dust. "Worked like a charm," he said, obviously pleased with himself.

"That was—," Kyle started, but he giggled too hard to finish.

"Amazing," I said, beginning to grin, and Prank looked as proud as Button had the night before. "How long until we can try it again?"

12
Peter Tries to Battle before Breakfast

J'd been looking forward to telling everyone else about our early-morning adventures, but something very weird was going on when we got back to the Tree Home—weird even for Neverland. Peter, Button, and Dibs stood in a line in front of their home, their swords drawn. Tink looped and dived through the air around them, hissing and shaking her little fist.

All four of them were obviously ready for a fight.

The weird part was that I didn't see anyone for them *to* fight.

"Have at thee, villains!" Peter cried. "This is our home, and we will die defending it!"

Button and Dibs exchanged glances, looking a little

queasy. It didn't seem like they wanted to die defending anything.

"Does Peter have some invisible enemies?" I asked, looking around.

Kyle shook his head. "It's the Never birds."

I squinted at the ground in front of Button and Dibs. Then one of the Never birds flapped its wings with an angry squawk, and I saw where they were standing, ten of them. Their feathers blended into the dark brown soil so well that it was easier to see their shadows stretching out behind them than the birds themselves.

As Prank, Kyle, and I landed in the clearing, Button smiled. "You're back."

"Just in time for the battle," Peter said, saluting us with his golden sword.

"Battle?" I said, eyeing the Never birds skeptically. I was starting to get the impression that Peter just liked to fight.

But the Lost Boys didn't really act like it was out of the ordinary. They didn't even seem all that excited. Maybe they were used to fighting random battles as soon as they woke up, and this was just part of their daily routine.

Prank placed the bucket full of fairy dust carefully at the base of the Tree Home. "Just a sec. Let me get my swords." He flew up toward his hiding place.

"Do you want to fight too?" Kyle asked me. "I don't

think they'll need us, but I can get your sword if you want."

"Um . . ." To be honest, I didn't really want to.

The Never birds had just helped us out with the pirates the night before. Maybe we didn't always agree on where they should put their nests, but weren't the Never birds our friends?

"That's okay," Kyle said, guessing that I meant no. "I'll grab us breakfast, and we can watch from here." He flew up to the branch above the others' heads, where a bunch of muffins were balanced on two tray-sized leaves. Someone must've gone to get them from the Grove of Food Trees.

Kyle tossed me one.

It was slightly warm, like it had come fresh from the oven. "Thanks," I told Kyle, even though I wasn't completely sure I wanted to watch either.

The Never bird on the end ran sideways, closer to Kyle and me, and stopped, looking us up and down. I noticed the mark on her beak. It was Spot, the bird who filled her nest with rocks, the one younger than all the others.

She took another hesitant step closer. I was sure of it now. She was staring at *me*.

"How dare you, scoundrel!" Peter told the bird, flying to my rescue. "Attacking our unarmed Wendy girl!"

But the young Never bird didn't *seem* like she was attacking. She was just looking at me—or rather, at the muffin that was in my hands.

With a cry, Peter raised his sword over the Never bird in front of me, preparing to strike.

"Objection!" I cried. Then I remembered that Peter might not know what that meant. "I mean, wait! Please!"

To my surprise, Peter blinked at me, looking startled. "But why?"

"Maybe we can solve this without fighting," I suggested. Peter frowned, eyeing Spot uncertainly. This was clearly a new idea for him. "Let's reexamine all the evidence. I don't think they want to hurt us." I turned to Spot. "Is that true? Do you want to fight? Shake your head if the answer is no."

Spot swung her beak from side to side.

"See?" I told Peter. "I'm sure we can find a diplomatic solution."

Looking stern, Peter squared his shoulders and puffed up his chest. I'm pretty sure he was Pretending to be a diplomat. "You don't want to move back into our tree, do you? Because we can't allow that."

The Never bird shook her head again, and seeing what was going on, the rest of the Never birds and the Lost Boys crowded around.

"Then what is it that you *do* want, Spot?" I asked,

tossing my muffin from hand to hand. Spot's gaze followed it, and then she looked at me with a pleading look.

"This?" I said, surprised, holding up the muffin.

Spot nodded vigorously and squawked.

"Oh, they're hungry, that's all," I told Peter and the Lost Boys.

"Well, then, they'll have to fight us for it—for every last crumb," Dibs said savagely, but when no one else echoed him, he started to look a little unsure. "Right?"

"Do they have to?" I asked Peter. "We already moved them out of their tree. Can't we share a few muffins?"

Peter considered, pacing the air a few inches above the ground.

The Never birds looked up at him pitifully. The Lost Boys (well, except for Dibs) looked at him hopefully, lowering their swords.

"As long as the Never birds do not try to move back into our tree," Peter said in a firm, diplomatic voice, "then they may eat."

Honking with delight, the Never birds launched themselves into the air. They landed on the branches around the leaf tray and picked at the muffins.

"Here you go," I told Spot, holding out my muffin before she flew off too. She ate it in two gulps and then rubbed her head affectionately against my legs, the same way a cat might. I smiled, petting her feathers. "You're welcome. I'm not sure if I would've wanted to fight before I'd eaten anything either."

"There's just one problem," Dibs pointed out, glaring at me like it was my fault. "The Never birds are eating *all* the muffins. We won't have enough for *our* breakfast."

The Lost Boys all turned to me. Peter turned too, suddenly looking less like a diplomat and more like someone who just found out that he might have to skip a meal.

"Maybe we can eat out?" I suggested hopefully.

When we reached the Grove of Food Trees, Tiger Lily and her braves were already there. They greeted Peter and the Lost Boys enthusiastically.

"Hello! Good morning to all of you!"

"Button, my pudgy friend, you must sample this fruit tart."

"You haven't run into pirates today, have you?"

"They've been searching the wood for Hook's hat."

"There it is. Dibs, did you steal it?"

"No, it must've been Peter. Or Prank."

None of them noticed me, but I didn't mind all that much. I needed a second to take in the scene around me.

Tiger Lily's tribe wasn't what I expected. The princess herself wore blue and red beads and feathers and soft doeskin leggings. She looked so beautiful and so polished that every time I glanced at her, I felt self-conscious about my torn and dirty pajamas.

Her braves were another story.

They talked with faint *English accents* and wore the most random outfits: one brave wore an orange leather jacket with green gym shorts; another wore a ripped tuxedo with bright beaded necklaces and no shirt; several just wore faded plaid shirts and cut-off jeans.

Really, the only sign that they all belonged to the same tribe were the feathers braided into their long hair and the war paint on their faces.

And then there were the food trees. I didn't see any apples and pears or fruits like that. Instead, whole meals grew on the branches. On one tree, french fries hung ripening in clusters like grapes, and cheeseburgers dotted the tree next to it. One smallish tree looked like it was covered in huge ripe oranges, but when I got closer, I saw that they were actually balls of macaroni and cheese. From another, cupcakes hung upside down from stems like apples.

One tree was covered with tiny pizzas, all different kinds—four-cheese, sausage with red peppers, supreme, a few with mushrooms, one with just broccoli (eww!). The tree even had Mom's favorite: half pepperoni and half pineapple with onion. I wondered how the cheese and toppings stayed on them, but magic must've kept them from sliding off.

I reached up, picked a mini pizza off the tree, and nibbled thoughtfully. It was delicious—much better than my last pizza at home!

With my food in hand, I glanced around the grove for a place to sit. No one looked my way.

Peter was telling the story about Hook's hat to six or seven braves, with Tink and Dibs acting out all the scenes.

Under the cheeseburger tree, Button sat with a brave wearing a camouflage T-shirt torn at the shoulder. It looked like he was teaching Button how to make an arrow while they ate.

Since the braves couldn't fly, Prank and Kyle did them a favor and picked food off parts of the tree that the others couldn't reach.

"Would you mind getting me that cupcake, Kyle? No, not that one. The one on the right. That's the one," said one brave.

"Prank, if you could possibly reach that pizza . . . ?" said another.

I stopped in my tracks. It suddenly felt like when you go to the cafeteria on the first day of school—not knowing where to sit or where you belong.

Tiger Lily! I could sit with her!

I flew up into the air a few feet and searched the grove for the princess.

There she was, across the clearing, between the macaroni and cheese tree and the cupcake tree.

She had the same look as the most popular girl in school. She didn't dress like anyone else. She dressed better—the deerskin gown fit her exactly; the beading stitched on it shone in the sun. The feathers and beads braided in her hair were like carefully chosen accessories. She looked over the scene with a calm, cool confidence. She was royalty, and she knew it.

Then she glanced in my direction. I was almost sure of it. I smiled and flew toward her.

But right before I landed, she turned away and started talking to the brave beside her.

Surprised, I abruptly lost my happy thought.

I fell to the ground so fast that my heels stung.

I really *wanted* to think that she just hadn't seen me. She *was* the only other girl in the grove. Wouldn't she want us to stick together?

It certainly didn't look that way.

Maybe Tiger Lily didn't want to be my friend.

"Wendy girl! Come over here! I want you to meet someone," Kyle shouted.

He was sitting at the base of a tree covered with chicken tenders that hung in bunches like bananas.

The smallest brave knelt next to him. He wore a

sleeveless shirt, which showed off the red stripes painted all the way down his arms. He had also painted a red smiley face on his cheek, which didn't seem very warlike.

I flew over, grateful that *someone* wanted my company. "Hi."

Smiling, the little brave moved his bow and quiver out of the way so that I could sit down beside them. "I am Pouncing Squirrel," he said with a deep nod. He had an English accent too, but he sounded a lot more formal than the others.

Personally, I thought that if he was going to be a brave, he was going to need a name more intimidating than Pouncing Squirrel, but it would've been rude to say so. "Nice to meet you. I'm Ashley."

"A pleasure," said Pounce.

"He's Tiger Lily's brother," Kyle told me, and he took a huge bite of his cheeseburger. Pounce gave Kyle a sharp look. I guessed he didn't like to be introduced like that. "The second in command among the Indians. What is it that you guys call yourself now?" he asked the brave. "The Forest Walkers?"

"Nah, that was last week," said Pounce. "Now, we're the Cubs."

"Like bear cubs?" I asked, confused.

Pounce shook his head. "Like *Tiger* Lily's Cubs."

"Not buds? Or seedlings?" said Kyle in a sly, teasing

way, and I pressed my lips together, not wanting to laugh in case it offended someone.

"Yeah, right—how scary would that be? Tiger Lily and her Fearsome Seedlings!" said Pounce. To me, he said, "Kyle has been telling me of your adventure. I am very impressed."

I smiled, feeling proud of myself. I'd already had a *ton* of adventures. "Which one exactly?"

"The fairies, this morning," Kyle said through a mouthful. "Pounce and I tried once before."

"I wanted some fairy dust. To be the first brave to fly in Neverland," said Pounce. "Kyle offered to help me. Unfortunately, it did not go as we hoped."

"That's why Prank didn't want to bring me," Kyle explained. "The fairies knocked us both off the cliff."

"Without fairy dust," Pounce added with a rueful smile.

"Ouch," I said with a wince. That cliff was pretty tall.

"We climbed back up—the hard way," Kyle said. He and Pounce exchanged glances and smiled at the memory.

"I have also heard that you stole Hook's hat, Wendy girl," Pounce said. "That is a great feat."

I'm a sucker for compliments, just like the rest of them. Right then, I decided that Tiger Lily didn't see me earlier. She couldn't be so mean, not with a brother as friendly as Pounce.

Just as I glanced around, looking for her, the princess slipped into the trees at the edge of the clearing. She carried her bow and quiver across her shoulder.

I jumped to my feet. I didn't want her to leave before I tried making friends one more time. "Where's Tiger Lily going?"

Pounce shrugged. "Who knows? She is very odd, my sister."

"Quick—what's her favorite food here?" I asked.

"Cupcakes," said Kyle.

"Her tooth is quite sweet," Pounce agreed. "Why do you ask?"

"I'm going to bring her some," I said, running to the cupcake tree. I picked off a tray-size leaf and loaded it up with half a dozen cupcakes, all different kinds, hoping that Tiger Lily would like one of them.

Kyle and Pounce exchanged another look. This time they didn't smile. "I don't know if that's such a good idea," said Kyle.

"She's *proud*, my sister," Pounce said in a warning way. But I didn't listen to them any more than I'd listened to Peter about the mermaids. I was *determined* to get on the princess's good side.

"I have a plan," I reassured them, and, rising into the air, I flew after Tiger Lily.

13
The Pirates Want My Cupcakes

*M*y plan had one major problem.

I couldn't find her.

Balancing the leaf tray of cupcakes carefully, I flew one way and came to a cliff—a dead end. I turned back and went another way, passing huge, towering trees with flaking gray bark. Their branches were covered in so many leaves that I couldn't see anything beyond them.

I was so disappointed at not finding Tiger Lily that I had a hard time holding on to my happy thought. My toes brushed the forest floor as I flew. Too bad everything wasn't as easy as fighting with a sword and faking a thunderstorm. . . .

Suddenly, I had an idea.

I landed on the nearest branch, closed my eyes, and Pretended that I was *already* Tiger Lily's friend. I Pretended that I already knew her so well that I knew exactly where to find her.

Then, suddenly, like someone had whispered the answer in my ear, I *did* know.

I flew past seven trees and circled the last one's trunk. There, crouched low between the exposed roots, was Tiger Lily. She didn't see me. This time I was 100 percent positive. Her head was tilted slightly, as if she was listening to something in the distance.

"Hi!" I said, very pleased with myself.

Tiger Lily jumped a foot and a half. Obviously, she hadn't been expecting me. *"Silence!"* she hissed, her eyes very wide.

I tried again, lowering my voice to a whisper. "Listen—I brought you some cupcakes. Want some?"

She scowled. It actually looked pretty intimidating with all the war paint on her face. "You foolish Wendy girl, can't you hear the pirates?"

"The pirates?" said a sea-roughened voice behind us. "You wouldn't mean us, would you, Princess Tiger Lily?"

I whirled around.

Five pirates circled us, grinning, only a few feet

away. Their drawn swords gleamed even in the shadows of the great trees overhead. Up close, I could see the holes in their clothes and the gaps where teeth were missing. I could even smell them—a mixture of saltwater, sweat, and something else unpleasant, like very bad breath.

"And who's this?" asked the same pirate who had spoken first, the one in the yellow-and-blue striped shirt. He took a step closer, staring at me. "Have you made a friend, Tiger Lily?"

Tiger Lily didn't answer. She drew an arrow out of her quiver, holding it near the top like a dagger, and with her other hand, she picked up a stout clublike stick from the forest floor. She was obviously prepared to fight.

I definitely wasn't. My heart thudded in my chest, and the blood rushed in my ears.

It's one thing to come up with a plan to scare off pirates when you're safely up a tree with four Lost Boys, one fairy, and one Pan as backup. On the ground, totally surrounded by pirates, it was almost impossible.

"Look at them little cakes," said a pirate behind the one in front. He dipped the tip of his sword into a cupcake on my leaf tray, and then, smirking at us from under his red cap, he licked the chocolate icing straight off the rusty blade.

I won't lie. I did want to fly away. But I couldn't just abandon Tiger Lily—not when I'd led the pirates straight to her.

"Yeah—where did you get that food, missy?" asked the pirate in the striped shirt. "You didn't nick it from our cook again, did you?"

"First the cap'n's hat, now our food," said another pirate, clucking his tongue. It was the short chubby one from yesterday—Smee.

I tried to Pretend to be a warrior, the kind that struck fear into pirates' hearts. It didn't work. It was hard to make-believe you were fearsome when holding six cupcakes instead of a sword.

"Do you know what the punishment is for stealing from pirates, missy?" asked Stripes, raising his sword. *"Death."*

Tiger Lily raised her stick, preparing to block the blow.

I couldn't let her fight alone. She was completely outnumbered. I had to do *something*. I *had* to help.

"The Sixth Amendment in the Bill of Rights clearly states . . ." It just popped out. My voice was a little squeaky. Scrambling to come up with a plan, I took a deep breath and continued, "'In all criminal prosecutions, the accused shall enjoy the right to a speedy and public trial, by an impartial jury—'"

Mouth open, the pirate in front lowered his sword,

and behind him his shipmates all raised their eyebrows.

"What's a Bill of Rights?" asked one.

"What's a jury?" asked another.

"What are you talking about?" ask Smee, sounding very suspicious.

I gained a little more confidence. "What I mean is, you can't convict someone of a crime without any evidence," I said, and my voice wasn't as squeaky.

The pirates were even more confused. They just kept gaping. Even Tiger Lily stared at me with a small, puzzled frown.

"What's evidence?" asked the red-capped pirate.

"Proof," I said.

"What about all the food?" said Stripes, but he was starting to sound a little unsure.

"Circumstantial," I said loudly. Mom used that word a lot when she talked about work. I wasn't completely sure what it meant, but it sounded so impressive that the pirates paused, looking at each other.

"Your lot stole our dinner from us yesterday," said Smee. "That's what our cook said."

"Yes, but does your cook usually make this kind of food?" I made a big show of looking down at the leaf tray in my hands. "A cupcake with sprinkles and pink icing? That doesn't seem very piratey."

All Hook's men lowered their swords. One even scratched his head.

"I guess there's no help for it," said Smee. "We'll have to take 'em to the cap'n. He can sort out this evidence and jury business."

That was such a happy thought that I rose an inch off the ground. Being captured was better than being killed. We would have a better chance of escaping.

But then another voice came out of the forest. "Smee? Is that you?"

I didn't recognize the voice—I had only heard Hook speak once before—but the pirates knew it right away. They all straightened up, doing their best to look scary again.

"Yes, Cap'n," said Smee. "What are you doing off the ship, Cap'n, sir?"

My heart sank, and so did I, as my happy thought drained away. I had the feeling that Hook would be much harder to trick, and Tiger Lily and I didn't have time to get away.

The princess tightened her grip on her weapons, determined to go down fighting.

"Smee, you fool, come and help me," said the voice.

"We have two prisoners here for you, Cap'n," Smee replied.

All of a sudden, a roar filled the air. To our right, leaves rustled like a huge animal was crashing around out there.

The pirates froze, gulping.

Even Tiger Lily shifted nervously on the balls of her feet.

I stared at the woods in horror, remembering the carving Button had shown me the night before. "Are there *real* lions in Neverland?"

"Never mind them, Smee," cried Hook's voice, a little shriller now. "It's coming!"

Then there was another roar, and then branches snapped violently, as if the lion was starting to chase its prey.

"Smee!" cried Hook's voice, fainter than before, like he was running away.

The pirates bolted, disappearing into the woods in every direction. Only Smee loyally ran in the direction of Hook's voice.

Hearing the roar, Tiger Lily and I backed up as much as we could. We pressed ourselves flat against the tree trunk and hoped the lion wouldn't notice us.

But a lion never arrived.

Instead, Dibs, Kyle, Button, Prank, and Peter emerged from the leaves, grinning from ear to ear. Tink zigzagged around their heads, chittering smugly, as if she knew all along that I would get in trouble by myself.

Tiger Lily's mouth fell open.

"Oh." My knees went a little weak with relief. "Was it just you guys?"

To answer, Peter opened his mouth and let out a very realistic lion roar.

"And I did the other parts," said Dibs with Hook's voice, obviously pleased with himself. "I can imitate that ugly old pirate almost as good as Peter."

"We would've attacked earlier," said Button apologetically, "but we all left our swords at our tree. We don't usually need them right after breakfast."

"Tricking works too," Peter said with a little shrug.

"But I can't remember the last time we tricked the pirates two days in a row," Kyle said, excited.

"And I know just who's responsible," Prank said, sweeping forward and shaking my hand heartily. "Our own Wendy girl, the most cunning lady to ever visit Neverland."

With a little laugh, I turned to grin at Tiger Lily, but she didn't really look relieved. She just looked mad—and actually, even scarier than before.

She thanked Peter with a deep nod, and then she started off through the woods toward the Grove of Food Trees and her own tribe. She glanced back only once—glaring at me so fiercely that I fell back a step.

I didn't understand it. We had just defied pirates side by side—the same way Pounce and Kyle had fallen off a cliff together. Why couldn't Tiger Lily and I be friends after this?

We watched her go. Then Kyle whispered, "I don't

think that she likes being rescued very much."

But I remembered what Pounce had said earlier—*she is proud, my sister*. He had *tried* to warn me.

I swallowed hard. Tink still didn't like me. The mermaids didn't want to be my friends, and now, Tiger Lily had just snubbed me. Well, that settled it. Maybe Peter was right. Maybe all my plans for this trip to Neverland weren't very smart.

The Lost Boys like you, though, I reminded myself firmly, before I started to feel *too* sorry for myself. *So you've made* some *friends.*

"Well, *I* certainly appreciate getting rescued," I said with feeling, and Peter and the Lost Boys grinned at me.

"You can thank us with cupcakes. Rescuing always makes me hungry," Prank said, picking one up from the leaf tray I was still holding, and he took such an enormous bite that he smeared yellow icing on his chin. "Who else wants one?"

14
A Crocodile Sings Christmas Carols

"Time to finish the spring cleaning," Button said a few minutes later, licking the last cupcake crumbs off his fingers.

"I thought we did that yesterday," I said as we rose in the air to fly back. "What else do we have to do?"

Apparently, now that the Never birds were out of the way, we had to wash the Tree Home from crown to roots.

Kyle scrubbed the outside of Peter's little red house, paying special attention to the windows. Button swept the stairs and checked to make sure the vine netting around each of the leaf hammocks wasn't fraying.

Peter disappeared into his house.

The rest of us got stuck wiping down the leaves with damp rags.

I know that I had already had a couple of adventures that morning, but cleaning a tree was *not* how I'd pictured spending my second afternoon in Neverland. And the whole thing with Tiger Lily was still bothering me.

"Is this really necessary?" I asked finally, after I had cleaned so many leaves that I had lost count.

"Peter's orders," Dibs said. That was apparently all the reason he needed.

I was instantly suspicious. What *was* Peter doing inside? For all I knew, Peter could be napping while the rest of us cleaned.

Prank rubbed down a leaf as long as his arm. "We've lived here for so long that we've covered the whole tree in fairy dust. See it on the leaves?"

I did see it. I'd noticed it the day before, too. It made the tree glitter in the sun, at least on all the leaves that we hadn't wiped down yet. "Yeah. But why are we washing it off? Are you afraid that the tree's going to have a happy thought and fly away?"

Prank shook his head and moved on to another leaf. "If the pirates ever notice, they'll know it's ours. We can't take any chances now that they're roaming the woods, searching for Hook's hat."

"They didn't find us last night."

"It was almost dark," Prank said.

"Maybe there's something we can do to make cleaning more exciting," I said hopefully. "You know, like the contest yesterday with the Never birds. What if we raced?"

Prank shook his head. He concentrated on the leaf he was cleaning as hard as he had when he'd organized the fake thunderstorm that morning, almost like this was just another trick. "We did that one year. We didn't do a good job, and the pirates ended up finding us anyway."

It definitely sucked. I only got to visit Neverland for a few days, and we were spending most of them *cleaning*. The other Wendy girls had to be a bunch of pushovers if they just helped the Lost Boys do all their chores without a *peep* of protest.

"Wendy girl, if you're sick of wiping down leaves, I'm sure there's something else you could do," Dibs said.

I looked up hopefully.

Dibs flew down to a branch a little below us and scooped up a bundle of cloth piled against the trunk. I'd thought they were extra rags, since they were so frayed and dirty.

He shoved them into my arms. "You can wash the blankets."

Laundry would suck even more than cleaning the leaves, and from the smirk on Dibs's face, I guessed that he knew it. I could definitely add him to the list of the people who *still* didn't like me. I probably had a better chance of winning Tink over than Dibs.

I was about to complain, but then Button said, "Would you mind, Wendy girl? I was going to do it after I finished, but this is taking longer than I thought."

He sounded exhausted. I couldn't say no. *Button* had always been so nice to me.

"Thanks," he said, and I could tell he really meant it. "I usually take them down to the waterfall." Button pointed. "There's a path over there."

So, I flew down a well-worn path with a bunch of smelly blankets in my arms. I could only find *one* happy thought to keep me in the air—I didn't have to work with Dibs anymore.

When I heard water crashing up ahead, I knew I was getting close, but that didn't prepare me for how spectacular it was.

The waterfall wasn't that big—barely twice as tall as I was, and maybe two-and-a-half feet wide—but it made a merry sound. The water fell fast over the sparkling rocks, throwing up so much spray that it made little rainbows. Very green vines bordered it on each side, covered all over with red and pink flowers. The waterfall pooled at the bottom and then flowed out quickly to meet the ocean.

I sat down on a sun-warmed rock with the bundle. The Lost Boys certainly didn't do their laundry often. The blankets were stiff with dirt, and I had no idea how to clean them.

First, I tried the simplest solution. I closed my eyes and Pretended that the blankets were already clean, dry, and folded. But I didn't feel a tingle even in my pinky toes.

That's the thing about Pretending in Neverland. It only works if you really *want* whatever you're make-believing. That meant I could Pretend to find Tiger Lily and to make thunder—but *not* to do laundry.

I sighed. It looked like I had to tackle the blankets the old-fashioned way. I picked up the whole pile, dumped it all in the pool, and poked at the blankets with a stick, kind of swirling the sodden cloth around a little.

"I can't believe it," I mumbled to myself. "One day in Neverland, and I'm already doing their laundry. I'm *not* their mother."

"That's not how Button does laundry," someone said.

Shocked, I nearly toppled into the water.

On the other side of the pool, sunning herself on a rock, was a mermaid. Her blond hair was so curly that it stuck out like a triangle around her head, and her green tail had silver and blue stripes running up the sides. She wore a shirt woven from seaweed, and tiny white seashells hung from the hem and the ends of her sleeves, which looked a little like lace if you squinted.

I couldn't believe my luck. A mermaid, sitting twenty feet away! And I hadn't even noticed.

"I saw you yesterday," I said quietly. "You're the one who waved."

I really wanted to swim over to her rock. After all, this was my chance to make friends with a mermaid, but I felt much shyer than usual. I mean, Tink, Tiger Lily, and Dibs hadn't liked me. I'd started to think that as a Wendy girl, I wasn't friend material, at least in Neverland. I didn't *want* Peter to be right about that, but I was kind of afraid he was.

The mermaid only smiled. She certainly *seemed* friendlier than the princess.

"My name's Ashley."

"I'm Buttercup." Some people have a gravelly voice, but this mermaid actually had a *gurgly* voice. Every time she spoke, it sounded a little like someone blowing bubbles in their milk with a straw.

Peter had talked about the mermaids drowning people, but I had a hard time imagining Buttercup hurting someone. "You know Button?"

Buttercup nodded. "He's the one who taught me

how to speak human. He comes here sometimes with the laundry."

"How does Button do it, then?"

"I'll show you."

The mermaid slid into the water with only a very small splash. She grabbed a blanket underwater with her webbed hands. Then she twisted it very tightly, hit the bundle with a rock a few times, so hard that I saw bits of dirt float off. Next she shook out the blanket, twisted it up, and hit it again with the rock, knocking more dirt off.

"Just like that," she said, passing the twisted blanket and the rock to me.

Glumly, I banged the rock against the blanket and watched more grime float off.

Buttercup grabbed another one of the blankets and started washing it. I'm not sure what amazed me more: the fact that I was doing laundry with a mermaid, or the fact that someone would do chores when she didn't have to.

"You don't mind it?" I asked Buttercup, still feeling shy. "Cleaning, I mean."

She glanced at me out of the corner of her eye, and I realized she might feel shy around me, too. That made me feel much better.

"We mermaids don't clean, you know. We live in the water. It doesn't make sense to wash. Cleaning is kind of fun, because I've never done it before."

I thought for a second. "I've actually never washed my clothes by hand before either. At home we have a washer."

"A wash-her?" the mermaid repeated skeptically.

"You know, a machine," I explained. "You put clothes in it, and some soap, and you turn it on. Then you can come back later, and the clothes are all clean."

"Ma-chine?" Buttercup said.

She was just repeating everything I said. It made me wonder if mermaids might be . . . well, a little slow. Then I remembered what Peter had said right after I met him, and I snorted softly.

"This is magic where you come from?" she asked.

I nodded. "Magic. Or machinery." I didn't want her to ask me what machinery was, so I quickly added, "I've never done laundry with a mermaid before either."

She smiled, wider than before. Her teeth shone extra bright, like pearls. "You know mermaids don't usually get along with Lost Boys. Or their Wendy girls."

Maybe she was trying to tell me that she wasn't allowed to hang out with me. "But you're friends with Button," I pointed out hopefully.

"Yes, but no one knows about it. It's a secret."

"Oh! Then I won't tell, I promise," I said, and Buttercup smiled again, gratefully.

So Peter didn't know *everything*. Maybe a Wendy girl *could* make friends with a mermaid, after all.

We worked in silence for a while. The more I hit it, less and less dirt came free of the fabric, and when I couldn't see any more dirt come off, I started on another blanket.

By the third blanket, I had fallen into a rhythm. Buttercup started humming, and since her song seemed so familiar, I joined in. Then we started hitting the blankets in time to the music, and when we caught ourselves striking rock against fabric in unison, Buttercup and I grinned at each other.

It did start to feel kind of fun—much more fun than it might have been if I were alone, anyway.

The sound of sleigh bells came over the water. Hearing them, I recognized the song we were humming.

I stopped myself and turned around. "Where's that music coming from?"

"Him, probably," Buttercup said, pointing toward the ocean. At the mouth of the river, a huge and leathery creature swam. Only a few bumpy ridges were visible above the water. "He used to tick like a clock, but he's been singing since yesterday. Very strange. Very sudden."

The music got a little louder, and I could hear the words "Jingle all the way!"

Then the crocodile surfaced, lifting its head out of

the water, and I saw the scar around its slitted eye and the row of enormous yellow teeth.

"Yesterday, he swallowed my mother's iPod!" I watched the crocodile's head fall back into the sea.

"Eye pod?" said Buttercup. "What's that? Is it like glasses? Button says he needs glasses."

I shook my head. "It makes music. I think 'Jingle Bells' must be playing on repeat."

As if it could sense us, the crocodile started swimming upstream, slowly and purposefully.

I gasped, scrambling back from the rock, away from the water. "Buttercup, get out of the water! It's coming this way!"

The mermaid looked up, drenched blanket in one hand and rock in the other, watching the crocodile come closer and closer.

"Buttercup, hurry!" I cried, running forward to drag her to safety.

But instead of hurrying, Buttercup did a strange thing. She slid deeper into the water until her mouth was covered, and she began to hum, the same way that the mermaids had done the morning I arrived in Neverland, right before the huge wave splashed Tink.

I couldn't hear her very well over the sound of singing, but apparently, the crocodile did. It slowed, stopped, and finally turned around, swimming back to the ocean like it was in a daze. Buttercup didn't stop humming until it was out of sight.

My mouth was open, and I closed it with a snap.

Buttercup laughed. Or at least she smiled really wide and made an extra-loud gurgling sound, which I assumed was how a mermaid laughed.

"He never bothers the mermaids," she said, rising from the water and taking a seat on the rock with a tiny, smug smile. "We have our own ways of dealing with him."

"That's so cool," I said. "Can you teach me?"

Her smile started to look a little apologetic. "I don't think magic can be taught, not to a human." I must've looked disappointed, because she added, "But maybe I can get you a trident. That's what we use when he's extra hard to manage."

I perked up. A trident would be cool.

Buttercup looked over my shoulder, toward the path that led back to the Tree Home. "Someone is coming," she said, dumping the blanket she'd been cleaning and the rock onto the shore. "I have to go, Ashley."

"See you soon!" I said quickly, hoping that it would be true. She was the first person in Neverland to call me by my name.

She slid under the water and started to swim out to the ocean, the way the crocodile had gone.

"Wendy girl!" shouted a Lost Boy behind me. I turned. Kyle glided through the trees. "I finished early, so Peter said to come and help you!"

"Great!" I called back, picking up the half-cleaned blanket Buttercup had left behind. Looking downstream, the way she had gone, I wondered if I *would* ever see her again. I hadn't even gotten the chance to thank her.

Peter Gives Me a Tour of His House

When Kyle and I got back with the clean blankets, I figured out a much better method for drying them than spreading them out in the sun like Button usually did. Better, as in much more fun. This time, I actually convinced the Lost Boys to try it.

We flew races with the blankets tied around our necks like capes.

Whoever lost the last round had to play referee for the next. Most recently, that had been Dibs, and he wasn't too happy about it. He watched us sourly from the finish line, which Button had scratched in the dirt with a sharp stick.

"On your mark!" Dibs called.

Across the clearing, Kyle, Prank, Button, Tink, and I all stood on the same thick branch on the Tree Home. (Peter still hadn't emerged from his house.)

"Get set!" cried Dibs.

Our blanket-capes flapped in the breeze. We leaned forward. The Never birds squawked encouragingly from the next tree.

"Go!"

We all jumped and flew as fast as we could.

Tink took the lead. As a fairy, she had more flying experience than me and all the Lost Boys put together. Of course, being a fairy also meant that her blanket-cape was way too big for her. One good gust of wind blew her off course.

That left *me* in the lead. I grinned and leaned forward.

"Wow, Wendy girl—your blanket's almost dry," said Prank right behind me.

"Really?" I turned to look.

But the second I started to slow, Prank zipped around me and zoomed ahead. "Fell for it!"

"Hey!" I cried, trying to catch up, but Prank had already crossed the finish line.

"I like this way of drying blankets much better than Button's," Prank said, turning to me with a huge, smug grin. "We should've gotten you for a

Wendy girl years ago."

It was hard to be mad at Prank after he said something like that. I'm pretty sure that's why he said it.

"Does that count?" Kyle asked, coming in right after me.

Button came in last, behind Tink. "I guess this makes me the referee again," he said sadly. "I'm not very good at racing."

"I could disqualify Prank," said Dibs. He sounded like he liked the idea.

I shrugged. "I mean, it's not like we set any rules."

Very wicked smiles spread across everyone's faces, and Tink rubbed her hands together gleefully. I started to worry that the next round would have more cheating than racing.

Unfortunately, I never got a chance to find out.

The door to Peter's red house banged open, and Pan himself emerged, his fists planted firmly on his hips. "All right—who wants to help me clean in here?"

Tink tossed her cape over the nearest branch and zipped over to Peter with a merry chime. It sounded a lot like "Me! Pick me!"

"Not you, Tink," said Peter. "You're too little."

The fairy stopped and drifted to the nearest branch with a sulky flicker.

Peter looked over at the rest of us.

All the Lost Boys shrank back, hanging their heads.

You would've thought that Hook had just asked who wanted to walk the plank.

Kyle even squeezed his eyes shut and whispered, "Please no more cleaning. *Please* no more cleaning."

"How about the Wendy girl?" Peter said.

I began untying my blanket-cape, trying not to pout. I didn't feel like cleaning anymore either, but I *would* get to see the inside of Peter's house.

"Bummer," said Prank with an apologetic sort of grimace. Button and Kyle nodded, looking sympathetic.

"Why?" asked Dibs. "She's a Wendy girl. Isn't cleaning what she's here for?"

I shoved the damp blanket-cape at Dibs. "Well, somebody still needs to dry this."

Quickly, I flew across the courtyard and past Peter, ducking my head through the red house's small doorway. Then I looked around eagerly.

Inside, Peter's house was bigger than it looked from the outside. Big enough for furniture. Not homemade Neverland furniture like the leaf hammocks that Button made, but *real* furniture: a small bed painted blue, a wooden nightstand with a lantern, a rocking chair set beside the fireplace, and a bookcase with lots of shelves. The striped wallpaper peeled in a few places, but the curtains in the window were very white, almost like they were new.

Strangest of all, it wasn't messy. Not a sock was on the floor; no pillow was out of place. I didn't even see any dust.

Confused, I turned to Peter. "But it's already clean."

Peter grinned as proudly as Prank did after he pulled off some great trick. "I know. I cleaned it already. But the Lost Boys aren't allowed in here. I tricked them so they wouldn't get jealous when I showed you around."

"Oh." I didn't mention that he had tricked me, too.

The inside of Peter's house didn't look too much different from my bedroom, or any other kid's my age. Besides the fact that it was in a tree, it looked pretty normal.

But in a weird way, I felt like I was looking at a secret. Even though he was famous, even though he had adventures that my friends at school never dreamed of, maybe he still wanted what other kids had. Maybe he was a little sick of adventures. Maybe, to Peter, having a normal life seemed more exciting.

"Where did all this come from?" I asked.

Peter shrugged, like it wasn't important. "Found it. This is what I wanted to show you," he said, motioning me toward the bookcase. "It all came from Wendy girls."

The shelves were cluttered with a strange bunch of stuff—a wooden badminton racket with broken strings, old playing cards yellowing at the edges, half a Frisbee with teeth marks, a very worn stuffed rabbit, an old-fashioned porcelain doll with glass eyes, a broken hula hoop, a deflated soccer ball. A very frilly apron hung from a peg on the side of the bookcase, covered in grass stains.

Looking at all of it made me feel very uncomfortable. I started going over what I'd put in my backpack, wondering what I could leave in Neverland.

Peter watched me eagerly, waiting for me to say something.

So I pointed to the object sitting on the very top shelf all by itself—a green acorn attached to a delicate silver chain. "What's that?"

"Wendy's acorn necklace. It saved her life," he said proudly. He reached up and took the necklace down, holding it carefully. It was obviously very special to him. He turned the acorn over so that I could see the crack in it. "Tootles—he was a Lost Boy then—he shot an arrow at her, and it hit her right in this very spot."

I gulped. "I'm glad that the Lost Boys like Wendy girls a little better nowadays."

"Well, it was Tink's fault. She told the Lost Boys to do it," Peter said, gently returning the necklace to its shelf.

I made a mental note to be more careful around Tinker Bell in the future. I mean, I already *knew* she didn't like me. But it was news that she could do something more dangerous than just pull my hair.

"And that," Peter said, pointing to a wicker basket on the bottom shelf, "came with the latest Wendy girl. The one who helped make the food trees."

I looked at it carefully. It was big enough for Kyle to fit into. So, Grandma Delaney *had* made the food trees. But I still had a hard time imagining her in Neverland, playing mother to the Lost Boys—she was so *old*.

"But this is what I wanted to show you," Peter said, reaching into the back of one of the middle shelves. He drew out a book. It was beat-up, but still kind of fancy. Even though the leather spine was cracked, the fairy etched on the cover was gilded.

"How pretty," I murmured, tracing the spine—*Children's Tales*, it said.

"I know you don't want to be a mother, but will you read the Lost Boys a bedtime story?" Peter asked hopefully, his eyes very wide. "The Lost Boys love stories."

I glanced up at Peter, startled. I had *not* been expecting him to ask me that.

My stomach knotted. It wasn't *exactly* guilt. I mean, I still definitely thought I would make a better friend than mother.

But like I said before, Neverland's magic only works

when you really *want* to become the thing you're Pretending to be. And even though I wanted to make the Lost Boys happy, I really *didn't* want to be like Mom. Even if I tried, I wouldn't feel even the slightest tingle.

"*Will* you read to them?" Peter said again, offering me the old book.

I nodded slowly, taking it from his hand with a tiny smile. I could tell them a bedtime story too—my *own* way. After all, I *could* Pretend to be the very best storyteller that Neverland had ever seen.

That night, while we ate pizzas that Button had picked for dinner, I read stories to the Lost Boys. And to Spot, who had smelled the food and flown down to beg for scraps. My fingers and toes started tingling as soon as I opened the book. I even made up voices for all the characters, which I thought was a nice touch, as I read "The Three Little Pigs," "Aladdin," and "The Nightingale."

I think the Lost Boys enjoyed the last one the most. The wheezy old-man voice I used for the emperor made them giggle. Peter got into the spirit too. He pulled out his pipes and played the nightingale's part, making up a tune whenever the bird sang in the story.

The Lost Boys listened without saying a word. Dibs sat in front, his eyes open very wide, the corners of his mouth curling up.

The sun went down halfway through the story, and Peter made Tinker Bell sit on my shoulder so I would have enough light to read by. Considering how much she hated me using her as a lamp the *first* time, the fairy wasn't thrilled. She crossed her arms and interrupted me with angry chimes, but once she noticed the illustrations, she didn't mind having a front-row seat.

"And they all lived happily ever after. The end," I said, a little hoarsely. "I think that's it for tonight."

I closed the book in my lap, and Peter took it out of my hands.

"Awwwww," Dibs said.

"One more," Kyle said. *"Please."*

"You know, I'm not the *only* one who can read these," I pointed out wryly. "Somebody else could take a turn."

The Lost Boys exchanged glances, and it occurred to me that maybe they *couldn't* read.

"Actually . . . ," Dibs said.

"We've forgotten how," Prank said with a shrug.

"Oh," I mumbled. None of them looked at all embarrassed about it, but my cheeks were definitely burning. "Sorry."

I felt so awkward about it that I started to reach for the book in Peter's hand, hoping that reading another story would make it up to them.

"No, we don't want her to read all of them," Button said. "She has to save some for tomorrow."

I smiled at him gratefully and rubbed my eyes. They felt kind of scratchy.

"Time for bed," Peter said firmly, and I felt pretty grateful to him, too.

"Wendy girl, will you tuck us in?" Kyle asked, flying up to his leaf hammock. "Please."

I stretched and rubbed my neck, sore after bending over a book so long. "I'm not sure that I know how."

"It's not hard," said Button, halfway up the tree.

"Kind of self-explanatory," said Prank in a hopeful way.

"But Mom *never* tucks me in," I said, and all the Lost Boys gasped.

"She never tucks you in, and then she *leaves* you?" Kyle said. It was obvious that he didn't like my mother very much.

I couldn't let them keep thinking that way about Mom. She wasn't as bad as I made her seem. I knew just what to do to change their opinion of her.

I flew up the tree and found Kyle's leaf hammock. He peered out at me curiously. "Okay, so maybe she doesn't tuck me in, but she always kisses me good night. No matter what. And she always kisses me good night exactly like this."

I leaned past the netting around his hammock and kissed his cheek. "One to kiss the bad dreams away." Then I kissed the other. "One to give good dreams." And finally, I kissed his nose. "And one to keep the fairies from carrying you off at night."

Tink chattered angrily. She apparently didn't appreciate me giving fairies a bad reputation.

I giggled. "Sorry, Tink, but that's how she does it. And she told me, *that's* how *her* mom kissed her good night when *she* was little."

The Lost Boys all became very still. Kyle's eyes were closed, and he smiled, his blanket bunched up in the crook of his arm like a teddy bear.

"Me, too?" Button asked hopefully from the next hammock over.

So, I kissed Button good night in the same way. And then Prank. And even Dibs, because it didn't seem fair to leave one Lost Boy out.

From the branch above Dibs's hammock bed, Tink chimed at me in a sharp way, but none of the Lost Boys were awake enough to translate for me.

"Did you want one too?" I asked, flying forward, but she jumped off the branch and flew into the forest.

Maybe Mom's good-night kiss speech had offended her more than I thought. Fairies *are* really touchy.

By the time I looked for him, Peter had already flown up to his house, which I took to mean that he

didn't want a good-night kiss either. But in the doorway, he turned and smiled at me with a half wave.

I climbed into my hammock, rubbing my eyes. I
knew one thing about bedtime stories and good-night
kisses. They made me miss my own mom a lot more.

16
I Rescue a Mermaid Princess

*W*hen I woke up the next morning, I was really confused. The last thing I remembered was a breeze whispering around my hammock, gently rocking me to sleep.

The breeze was stronger when I woke. It smelled salty, like the sea, which was a two-minute flight away from the Tree Home.

Then I heard a soft, questioning chitter and then a high-pitched hushing sound.

Instantly suspicious, I opened my eyes.

The sun sat on the horizon, just beginning to rise. I was in the middle of the ocean, so far away from shore that the trees looked tiny. White and purplish lights lined the edge of my leaf, chiming as quietly as possible. I recognized one of them.

"Tink! What are you *doing*?" I shouted.

The fairies were so startled that they dropped the leaf. My hammock bed plunged into the water.

An enormous splash came over the edge, soaking my pajama top. I shrieked, but the leaf was seaworthy. My hammock bed stabilized and floated as a swarm of fairies zipped around above my head.

It was easy to tell which one was Tink. She was chittering the loudest.

"Don't talk to me like that," I told her sternly. "I was *asleep*, minding my own business. You were the one caught in the act."

I don't think Tink wanted me to point this out, even if it was true. She dived at me, and I felt her tiny fingernails rake across my cheek. Her fairy friends followed her example, clawing at me so hard that I knew that some of them were drawing blood. I wasn't sure why *they* didn't like me, but maybe some of them recognized me from Prank's fake thunderstorm the day before.

I dived over the side of the leaf into the ocean, just to escape them, and I swam underwater a little way and surfaced at a safe distance from the fairy swarm, shouting, "I'll tell Peter!"

The fairies—in the process of hurtling toward me—froze in midair.

Tink's mouth slowly turned up at the corners, and she beamed an evil little smile at me. I knew instantly that she would get to Peter first and feed him some stupid story.

"Wait, Tink! Let's talk about this!"

But she and the rest of the fairy swarm were already zooming across the waves. In the dim predawn haze, they glittered over the ocean's surface like dancing Christmas lights.

I tried to launch myself into the air after them. I knew I had to have a lot of fairy dust on me after being carried halfway across Neverland, but I didn't lift an inch from the sea. Suddenly I remembered. Wet fairy dust didn't work.

There was no hope for it. I started to swim toward shore, trying not to think about the crocodile that sang Christmas carols or the story that Tink was telling Peter at that very moment. At least it was warm, I told myself. I would dry off pretty fast as soon as I got out of the water.

Then I noticed where Tink and her friends had been taking me. The *Jolly Roger* sailed along the shore, only a few hundred feet away. I froze, treading water, furious at myself for not seeing it before and furious at Tink for getting me into this situation in the first place. So much for winning over the fairy and becoming friends.

I watched the ship nervously. It wasn't that I was *afraid* exactly. But the run-in with the pirates the day before had taught me that Peter and the Lost Boys made pretty good backup.

The ship started to sail on by, and I breathed a sigh of relief. The pirates hadn't seen me. I was safe.

They passed close enough that I could hear the pirates laughing. "We've really got her now!" said a gleeful voice I recognized—Black Patch Pat.

Her? Did he mean Tiger Lily? Or Buttercup?

I spotted a rope hanging from the deck and made my way over to the ship, swimming quietly underwater as much as humanly possible.

The rope whipped through the water like a swimming eel. I grabbed it, and the speed of the ship almost pulled my arm from my shoulder. I hung on, even more determined to see what was going on. After a few false attempts, I pulled myself out of the waves.

I knocked against the side of the boat with a thump so loud that I was sure that someone had heard me. I paused, listening.

"Ask her again." The voice was as cold and slimy as the rope I was holding. It was Captain Hook. "Ask her again where Pan resides."

I kept listening as I shinnied up the slippery rope,

wishing that the fairy dust would kick in again. I didn't hear anyone answer, but there was this weird sputtering rasp.

"Cap'n, she still says she doesn't know," said another voice—Smee.

"Bring more wood. Stoke the fire," said Hook. "I *must* have Pan."

Soon, I reached the top. My hands curled around the rail of the ship. Slowly, cautiously, I peered over it, ready to dive back into the ocean if anyone looked my way.

A brazier was on the far side of the deck, and all the pirates had crowded around it, too absorbed to notice me. I couldn't understand why they would need a fire on such a warm morning. Orange flames fingered the grate as Black Patch Pat shoved a few sticks through the bars.

Then I saw her, hanging in a mildewed net, just a few feet above the fire. Buttercup.

Hook leaned toward her, pushing the net lazily so that she began to spin. "Now, my dear mermaid princess, once again, I ask you: where can we find Peter Pan?"

Buttercup looked terrible. Everything about her drooped. She didn't even raise her head as she rasped a few syllables.

I didn't think that she said anything, but apparently,

Smee understood her. "Still doesn't know, Cap'n."

"I bet she does," said another pirate, one I didn't recognize. "You can see it all over her scaly little face."

Buttercup choked on the rising smoke and started to cough, miserable. The ends of her blond curls were singed. Her lips were dry and cracking.

"I have been without my hat for two entire days, Buttercup," said Hook in his cold voice. "That is two days too long. Lower the net," he told his pirates.

Noodler let out a little rope. The net dropped. Buttercup squirmed, trying to twist away from the fire, but she couldn't get away. It was too close. The flames rose, as if trying to reach her.

This was torture! She didn't look like she was any older than me, but there she was. She rasped out the same noises over and over as loudly as she could, coughing from the smoke and struggling in the net. It must've been the mermaids' language.

It made me even madder to see the pirates just watching her gleefully.

"She still says she doesn't know," Smee told Hook.

My heart squeezed. Maybe she didn't know where the Tree Home was, but she *did* know where Button did the laundry. She could've told Hook, but she didn't. Buttercup was being very brave, and she was *definitely* being a good friend.

"You know, Cap'n—I've been thinking. She might

be telling the truth."

"Impossible," said Hook.

"Well, you know, Pan and the merfolk, they don't mix much," Smee pointed out. "Those mermaids, they have a terrible habit of trying to drown the Lost Boys. The one named Prank, in particular."

I knew one thing for certain: I had to rescue her. I didn't know if I could do it alone, but I didn't have time to go get the Lost Boys. It didn't look like Buttercup could last much longer.

For a second, the pirate captain looked disappointed. Then he straightened up, glaring at the mermaid slowly drying out over the fire. "She's the sister of the mermaid queen. She has to know *something*."

She made a loud rattling sound, like steam hissing from beneath a pot's lid.

I thought it was just a scream, but all the pirates became very still.

"Did she say what I think she said?" Black Patch Pat asked Noodler.

"Treasure!" shouted Smee triumphantly, and Hook's mouth curled under his black mustache.

"Where?" asked the pirate captain.

Buttercup began sputtering something, and Smee listened intently.

I would never be able to rescue her with all the pirates gathered around her. I glanced around for a distraction. The anchor hung over the ship's rail only a few feet from me. A lever stood beside it.

A plan started to form in my mind. Thinking about all the havoc it would cause made me so happy that I started to rise into the air. The fairy dust must have dried out—just in time, too.

I dashed forward and hit the anchor's lever with all my might.

The anchor *whish*ed as it plummeted toward the water and plunked when it plunged, but I didn't wait around to watch. I rushed around the ship toward my next target.

The anchor caught the ocean floor just as a couple of pirates heard my approach and started to turn my way.

The ship swung. The deck tilted wildly. Pirates flailed and fell. The brazier under the mermaid toppled. Hook fell against the helm and clung to it.

I flew into Noodler as hard as I could. Already unbalanced by the tipping ship, he stumbled and fell. I snatched up the rope that he dropped, the one attached to the net trapping Buttercup.

The force almost yanked me out of the air. "Whoa— you're *heavy*," I said to Buttercup.

The mermaid blinked wide, sea green eyes at me sleepily. I wasn't sure she recognized me. The smoke must have stupefied her.

"Who's *that*? Is there a new Lost Boy?" said a voice

behind us. The pirates had noticed me.

"Nah, that's the *Wendy girl*," said Smee. "The one who stole the hat off our dear cap'n's head."

"Get her, you dogs!" Hook shouted.

A bunch of pirates scrambled and slipped across the deck toward me.

With one hand, I pushed Buttercup past the side of the ship, over the water. We were still pretty high up, at least thirty feet, but I didn't have time to cut her free from the net. There wasn't any more that I could do. "I hope you can still swim," I told the mermaid, and I let go of the rope.

Buttercup and the net plunged into the ocean below. I zipped out of the pirates' reach as soon as I could, hovering anxiously over the water still churning from her drop.

"Man overboard!" someone shouted.

"Not *man*, pea brain. *Mermaid*," replied Black Patch Pat, peering over the side. "Mermaid overboard."

Bubbles and more bubbles rose to the surface, but no Buttercup. I swallowed, wondering if mermaids could drown.

"Salty Sal and Noodler, take off yer boots," said Smee. "You're the only ones who can swim. You're going in after her."

"No, no, no," Hook shouted. "Morons, the lot of you! Raise the anchor and right the ship first."

The ship wobbled a little in the water and stead-ied, perfectly level. Someone must have gotten to the anchor pretty fast.

I didn't know how long I had until the pirates started loading their cannons, but I didn't want to escape to the island before making sure my friend was all right.

"Buttercup!" I shouted, not even sure that sound carried underwater. "Buttercup, please!"

"Much better!" Hook said, practically singing. "Now, Smee, did the mermaid tell you the location of the treasure?"

"Yes, Cap'n. She certainly did, Cap'n."

"Then we have no reason to go after her. She has already told us everything she knows. Now, Smee, if you'll tell me the location of that marvelous trea-sure . . ."

Buttercup surfaced finally. Her lips were cracked and bleeding in two places, but she was smiling.

"You're okay!" I cried.

She said something to me, I was 100 percent sure. Her lips moved. But it didn't sound much different from the water gurgling through her webbed fingers.

"Buttercup, I can't understand you unless you speak my language," I reminded her.

"Oh," she said, and in English, I could hear how hoarse she'd become. "Ashley, you saved my life."

"We're not out of this yet," I told her, pointing to the ship.

"Right you are, Cap'n," we heard Smee say. "All right, men. To Queen Maris's palace—two minutes' swim from the fairies' tree along the coral reef, take a sharp right at the school of angelfish, and then veer left by Jellyfish Canyon—"

Buttercup hung her head, ashamed to have given away the mermaids' secrets. The water brought out all the green in her blond curls.

"What kind of directions are *those,* Smee?" growled Hook.

"They're the ones she gave me, Cap'n," Smee said, sounding a little unsure.

"Don't worry. It sounds like your directions might slow them down a little bit," I told Buttercup. "I think you should still warn the mermaids, though. Especially your sister."

When I flew toward shore, Buttercup swam just below me, looking unconvinced. "But they're going to be so *angry,*" she murmured. I had the feeling that she was worrying about Queen Maris's reaction the most.

"Well, if *I* were a mermaid, I wouldn't be as mad if you gave everybody a chance to prepare themselves."

Buttercup brightened up considerably. She waved me forward, smiling widely, and I leaned closer, expecting her to whisper something else in my ear.

Then she grabbed me around the shoulders. I stiffened, but it was just a hug. It was wet and smelled like seaweed.

She *did* gurgle something in my ear. It sounded a lot like the mermaid version of *thank you*.

As I watched her dive deep into the ocean and swim fast toward Mermaids' Lagoon, I felt something warm and tingly in my stomach, a new happy thought. Peter had been wrong. I *had* made friends with a mermaid.

Buttercup outstripped the pirate ship easily, but I saw Hook standing at the prow, watching her with a patient smile on his face. Smee stood beside him, screwing on a new hook, one with two points. Captain Hook was planning a battle. My new friend was in more danger than ever.

Well. He wasn't going to hurt *her*. Not if *I* had anything to do with it.

17
Tink Gets Banished

*K*yle noticed me first. As I flew into the clearing next to the Tree Home, he shouted, "The Wendy girl's back! She came back!"

Button and Prank whooped too, and landing, I looked at them, puzzled.

"Tink's been saying that you got scared—that you left in the middle of the night," Button explained.

It took me a second to remember back further than Buttercup's rescue. "Oh, right—I forgot that Tink would get here first." I spotted the fairy, sitting on one of the lower branches and glaring at me. She even had a tiny handkerchief raised dramatically to her face, as if blotting tears. I glared back at her, furious that she would go so far just to *fake* missing me. I had *tried* to befriend her. "Like she would be upset if I disappeared," I added, annoyed.

Dibs landed, the feather in Hook's hat windblown as if he'd been flying all over the island. "No sign of her. I *told* you she'd—," he started, both fists on his hips, but then he noticed me. *"Oh,"* he said, and sighed deeply, as if he had been hoping I was gone for good.

"I missed you, too, Dibs," I said sarcastically, and Dibs rolled his eyes.

"I *knew* you wouldn't leave without saying goodbye." Kyle took my hand and dragged me toward the Tree Home.

Peter stopped pacing the air beside Tink and stared at us. It surprised me when he smiled, relieved. I hadn't known that he would miss me if I left.

"Where *were* you?" he asked.

"At sea," I said. "Tink took me and my leaf on a boating expedition, but listen—"

Peter didn't listen. He turned furiously to the fairy.

"A boating expedition," Prank repeated appreciatively. It was the kind of trick that he daydreamed about.

"I knew it," Button said triumphantly. "She's done it before, but she hasn't done it since the original Wendy.

She must *really* not like you." He said it like a compliment.

The fairy dropped her handkerchief and flew around Peter's head. From the wailing pitch of her bell-like voice, it sounded like she was pleading her case.

"Tink, you are my friend no longer," Peter said fiercely.

I thought he was just exaggerating, but Tink took it very seriously. She started making these sharp little rings, like sobs.

"Wow, Peter hasn't said *that* since the first Wendy either," Button said, impressed.

"He must really *like* you," Kyle added.

That *did* feel like a compliment. I started to smile, but then Tink flew at me furiously. Ducking, I said, "That's very sweet of you, Peter, but I'm not sure it helps—"

Peter swatted at the fairy. "Begone from this place, Tink. I never want to see you again."

Tink let out a bell-like wail, half heartbroken, half outraged.

In a situation like this, I decided, it was best to just distract Peter. It would take the heat off Tink, and besides, Buttercup was still in danger. "The *Jolly Roger* is on the move," I told Peter.

He turned to me, eyes glittering, one hand on his sword hilt. "Hook?"

I nodded. "He wants the mermaids' treasure. He's headed for their palace."

"He can't be," said Button.

"He doesn't know where it is," Prank said smugly, as if he *did* know where it was.

"He does now. They all do," I said firmly. "Buttercup told him."

"She wouldn't," Button said slowly, looking horrified, and I remembered that he was Buttercup's friend too. "A mermaid work with a pirate?"

"No! They tortured her first." Button went very pale suddenly, and I added hastily, "She's all right now, though." Feeling anxious all over again, I turned to Peter. "Can we stop the *Jolly Roger*?"

A hush fell over the Lost Boys, a gleam of excitement in their eyes.

Peter fingered his sword hilt, looking thoughtful. He didn't answer.

Wanting to convince him, I almost added that Buttercup hadn't told the pirates where Button did laundry, but then I stopped myself. After all, I was sworn to secrecy about Button and Buttercup's friendship.

"If Buttercup's being tortured, shouldn't we rescue her first?" Button said, concerned.

"I already did that," I said.

Peter raised his eyebrows really high. "You did?"

"All by yourself?" Prank said, sounding impressed.

"The pirates are getting closer to the mermaids' treasure every second," I said impatiently. "*Please*, Peter. I'm worried about Buttercup."

"We've never helped the mermaids before," Prank added. "Could be fun."

Peter thought for a moment. The Lost Boys held their breath. Tink chimed uncertainly. I prepared to go by myself, but then the corners of Peter's mouth curled, very slowly. He drew his sword. "It sounds like a fine adventure!"

The Lost Boys cheered, and I hugged Peter around the neck before I could stop myself. He didn't mind, but Tink did. She grabbed my hair and yanked me back fiercely.

"Tink, I have banished you!" Peter shouted, shaking his sword at her. "Leave *now*, or I will chase you out."

With another ringing sob, she let me go and drifted into the forest. Even rubbing my sore scalp, I felt a little sorry for her, but the mermaids needed our help.

"Lost Boys! Weapons!" Peter shouted.

Button, Prank, Dibs, and Kyle flew to different spots on the trunk—their secret hiding places.

"I wouldn't bring that," Prank told Dibs, pointing at Hook's hat. "Not unless you want Hook to steal it back."

Dibs reluctantly took it off.

I flew up a few feet. "Kyle, do you still have my

sword?" I asked, beginning to pace the air, anxious to go.

"Got it!" Kyle raised the long thin blade that I had found among the blankets.

"Wait—*she's* coming?" Dibs asked Peter, shocked.

Like I said, *very* old-fashioned ideas about girls. But this time, only Dibs was thinking them.

I raised my chin defiantly. "What did you expect me to do? Wait here?"

"That's what all the other Wendy girls did," Dibs replied fiercely, glaring at me.

"You need to get out more," I said sharply. "Meet some people outside of Neverland."

"No, the Wendy girls came on adventures." Prank paused, thinking about it. "Usually, they came."

"Not with a sword, they didn't," Dibs grumbled, watching Kyle hand me mine.

"What was the point of teaching me to use it then?" I said, one hand on my hip and the other holding my sword.

"Do we really have time to argue?" Button asked. Prank hovered at his shoulder, carrying a sword in each hand.

We all turned to Peter. He looked at me in a long, measuring way. Then he rose into the air, and the Lost Boys followed. So did I, glaring at Dibs the whole time.

"She comes," Peter said finally. "If we tell her not to,

she'll only follow later."

I grinned. Peter really was starting to know me better.

Then he added, "This way, we can keep an eye on her and keep her out of trouble."

My grin faded. I thrust my face into the wind. I would prove to Peter that the only trouble I would bring was the kind I gave the pirates.

18
The Pirates Learn That I Am Not a Lady

The *Jolly Roger* moved quickly. By the time we burst out of the trees and flew over the waterfall, the pirate ship had already sailed past the spot where Buttercup and I had done laundry the day before.

"I don't see any mermaids," I said, hoping that my friend had warned them in time.

Peter didn't answer. None of the Lost Boys did. They all looked at the ship, grinning as we rushed over the water. Peter only had eyes for Hook.

The pirate keeping watch in the crow's nest noticed us first. It was Noodler. He yelled something, pointing up at us.

Peter crowed. It was the signal. The Lost Boys gave a great shout. I gripped the hilt of my sword tighter and joined them. We swooped down on the ship.

Kyle landed first and charged a pirate in a striped shirt, swinging his sword like a baseball bat. Prank was right behind him. He stood on the ship's rail, his chin lowered, and he raised both swords when four pirates came at him at once.

Dibs dashed down one side of the deck, striking at pirates as he went, and they turned and chased him. Button stood at the bow bashfully, holding his sword loosely at his side, gulping as he watched two pirates approach.

Peter didn't land. He just circled the pirate captain with a quiet, dangerous smile.

"Is it you, Pan, you insolent boy?" said Hook. "We were hoping you would show up."

"It's me, you old codfish," Peter replied, raising his golden sword.

I paused a second, hovering in the air, out of the pirates' reach. This was my first real battle. I wanted to do it right. I closed my eyes and Pretended as hard as I could: I was Ashley, the Wendy-girl Warrior, famed for her sword skills and feared by pirates.

Confidence flowed through me, and my sword felt more familiar in my hand.

Then, fingers and toes tingling, I landed among the remaining crew.

They stared at me in astonishment. I raised my sword, watching them all, ready for a fight.

"Ain't you the new Wendy girl?" asked one wearing a green cap.

"The one who saved the young mermaid princess?" asked another with missing teeth.

I grinned. "Of course I am."

All the pirates drew back a little bit. "Can't fight a girl," mumbled the one with the green cap.

"Not you, too!" I said, disappointed.

"Even if she does have a sword," agreed the one with missing teeth.

"Hey! That's *my* sword," Black Patch Pat cried indignantly.

"Finders keepers," I said smugly.

"Not fair," Black Patch complained, but I looked over his shoulder at the anchor's lever. If I couldn't fight any pirates, I might as well stop the ship.

I launched myself into the air and dived toward the lever, preparing to strike again.

A long dagger blocked my swing. It belonged to Smee, who peered at me through his glasses. "Oh no, you don't. Not again, missy," he said, so sternly that he reminded me of my mother. "You dogs," he said, turning to the pirates who wouldn't fight me, "what do you think you're doing, letting her go by?"

All the pirates mumbled excuses at once, so quickly and quietly that I couldn't understand any of it.

"I don't want to hear it," Smee said sharply. "We've got to keep this ship going. We need to reach the mermaids' palace."

"But *Smee*," said Black Patch Pat, "she be a *lady*."

"Lady or not, she be crafty," Smee replied. "The captain will not take it kindly if you let her stop the ship."

The three pirates turned to me with fierce scowls. I grinned and raised my sword again. They raced at me.

I swung at Black Patch Pat first and jumped up into the air again. The pirate with missing teeth stabbed wildly in my direction. I dodged and kicked at his arm so hard that he dropped his sword, howling in pain.

"Don't be such a baby!" said Black Patch Pat.

"She be stronger than she looks, she is," complained the injured pirate indignantly.

I grinned. I *was* good at Pretending.

I blocked a slice from the pirate in the green cap and kicked him in the stomach with as much force as I could muster. All the air went out of him with a grunt-like *oomph*. I started toward Black Patch Pat again, but then I heard a panicked shout behind me.

It was Kyle.

Four pirates had cornered him, and his sword was just out of his reach. Kyle grabbed a loose bit of rope and swung it at his attackers like a whip. The one on the right caught it and used it to yank Kyle toward him.

How dare those pirates single out the littlest Lost Boy! Why couldn't they pick on someone their own size?

I charged. The four pirates didn't see me coming. I pushed one into the other, and like dominoes, they all toppled.

"I didn't *need* help," Kyle said, getting to his feet, but he sounded a little shaky anyway. "I could've handled them."

"Right," I said with a small smile, passing him the sword that he'd dropped. Black Patch Pat and the four pirates after Kyle closed in again. I thought of a plan. "In the air, Kyle. Hold your sword in both hands again."

Kyle looked at me strangely, but he flew up off the deck, gripping his blade like I'd ordered. "Hold on to it," I warned him. I grabbed his feet and started to spin us around, so quickly that Kyle's sword swung out at our attackers.

When we stopped spinning, all five pirates were on the deck, moaning. Black Patch Pat's arm was bleeding.

I let Kyle go. He straightened up dizzily, still twirling a little in the air over the prow. "Whoa," he said, giggling. "That was *awesome*."

On the other side of the deck, Peter crowed. He

195

had cut off one big chunk of Hook's curly hair. The pirate captain grabbed the lock's shorn end in horror. I grinned, thinking that Hook was going to start *really* missing his hat.

"There she is!" shouted Noodler from the crow's nest. "Queen Maris's palace!"

My heart sank. "Keep an eye on that one," I told Kyle, pointing at a pirate who was starting to push himself to his feet.

"Yes, Wendy girl, ma'am!" Kyle replied cheerfully, saluting me.

I raced up, above all the pirates' heads, above the sails, above the crow's nest, glancing out over the water, looking for what the lookout saw.

At first, I didn't see any mermaids or anything like a palace. The sunlight reflecting off the ocean was too bright. Then the *Jolly Roger* moved forward slightly, and the ship's shadow fell across the water in exactly the right way.

Under the ocean's surface, all the towers in the mermaids' palace gleamed with mother-of-pearl, and schools of tropical fish swam around the entrance, as colorful as any banners. Mermaids streamed through the door, carrying shiny things in their arms—the treasure.

The *Jolly Roger*'s shadow crept over the palace slowly, and all the mermaids looked up at once. The one wearing a crown—Queen Maris—signaled. A dozen warrior mermaids swam forward, carrying gleaming tridents and wearing chain mail shirts made out of seashells. The one on the far right was Buttercup, looking fierce but pale. She hadn't recovered yet. She wouldn't last long in a fight.

I had to think of something fast.

I looked for Peter first. He was busy. Hearing that treasure was so close had put a gleam in Hook's eye and a spring in his step. He hacked at Peter with renewed energy, forcing Peter back. From the stubborn, angry look on Peter's face, I guessed he didn't like his retreat one bit.

The Lost Boys weren't faring very well either. Kyle was fighting again. A red-capped pirate knocked his sword from his hand a second time, but Kyle leaped up after it and caught the hilt in midair.

Button was occupying five pirates at once. Even though he was the biggest Lost Boy, he was the best at dodging. Not one of the pirates could touch him.

Dibs still had three pirates chasing him. They weren't close, but he was tiring, slowing down.

On the opposite side of the deck, Prank still wielded both swords with a merry mastery, but every time he disarmed one pirate, another one rose up in his place.

It confirmed my worst fear. We weren't going to overpower the pirates this way. They outnumbered us, at least three to one.

"Two hundred yards, Cap'n!" Noodler called, pointing from the crow's nest.

Smee pulled two pirates out of the melee with Button. "You two, ready the cannons. When we get in range, blast through the mermaids' defenses."

I looked wistfully at the anchor lever again. Peter and Hook were fighting directly in front of it—Peter on the offensive again, cartwheeling around the enraged pirate captain. I wouldn't be able to reach it.

There has to be some other way to stop this stupid ship! I thought, glaring furiously around the *Jolly Roger*.

Then I thought of it—*the sails.*

"Lost Boys!" I shouted, remembering how clumsy the pirates had gotten after I dropped the anchor earlier. "Brace yourselves!"

I raced up to the top of the mast. From the crow's nest, Noodler leered at me and raised his knife. I kicked at him, nearly knocking him over the rail, and turned my attention to the sail. I hacked at the rope that kept the canvas up, and the sail fluttered to the deck below. After my warning, the Lost Boys flew nimbly out of the way, but the pirates were too slow.

"I can't see!" shouted one, flailing under the thick canvas covering the whole ship. "I'm blinded."

Laughing, I cut the ropes for two other sails, and Prank—catching on faster than the others—soared up to cut down the last one. The *Jolly Roger* slowed and finally stopped.

"Cap'n, the mermaids!" shouted Smee from the only corner of the deck not covered with the sail. "They're getting away!"

"Smee!" said a tall bump under the canvas, quivering with rage as only Captain Hook could. "Cut. Me. LOOSE!"

The Lost Boys started a cheer. "Wendy girl! Wendy girl!"

I gave my sword a little twirl and smiled, pleased, when Peter started cheering too.

19

The Mermaids Invite Us to Dinner

*B*elow us, a mermaid surfaced with a splash. "Ashley," Buttercup cried, smiling widely.

Button abruptly stopped chanting and zipped toward her. "Are you all right, Buttercup?"

"Yes," Buttercup said. Peter, the Lost Boys, and I flew lower. "Thanks to Ashley. And all of you."

"It was the *least* we could do," Dibs said with a grand gesture. "I mean, we were the ones who stole Hook's hat and made him meaner than usual."

Annoyed, I thought, *You mean,* I *stole Hook's hat.*

Startled, I dropped a little lower in the air, dipping my toes in the sea.

That was right. *I* had stolen the hat. Did that mean that it was my fault Buttercup had been captured? I'd never heard of the pirates targeting the mermaids before, but what if they started doing it more and more now because of me? It was a terrible thought.

"Don't mention it," I said to Buttercup, squirming uncomfortably.

"Whoa," said Kyle. "A mermaid who can speak English."

"Or can you all do that?" Prank asked. "And have you been tricking us all this time?"

"No, just me." Buttercup's gaze slid to Button, who turned a little pink.

Peter looked between them with a small smirk, and I could practically see him working out their secret friendship. Button gulped, like he thought he would be banished along with Tink, but Peter just looked over at the cliffs behind us. "Our allies arrive!"

We turned. Princess Tiger Lily stood on the shore, the feathers in her hair dancing in the breeze. An arrow was notched in her bow, and, flanking her on both sides, her Cubs stood half hidden behind the huge tree trunks.

I waved with a huge grin. Tiger Lily hadn't been friendly the day before, but I *had* accidentally led the pirates straight to her. I couldn't blame her for being upset. But now I'd had my first real battle, and I hadn't done badly. Maybe that would win her over.

The princess didn't smile back.

"They're a little later than usual," Kyle murmured.

"It's not like we needed the help," Prank pointed out, jerking a thumb at the *Jolly Roger*. Its red sails were still draped over the dock, but they were full of holes now that the pirates had cut themselves free.

"How clever I am," Peter said, but he nodded my way, like he was complimenting *me*. "A very fine adventure."

I couldn't stop myself from rising giddily into the air.

I glanced back at the shore, but Tiger Lily and most of her tribe had disappeared.

Only one brave remained. Pounce. I recognized the red stripes painted down his arms. He raised both hands and shrugged, and then he too stepped back and faded into the shadows.

Something about the way they left and the way they had looked at us—very quiet and reserved—made me feel a little worried, but I couldn't figure out why.

We spent the afternoon escorting the mermaids to their new home, a cove on the other side of the island. It took them a few trips to move all their treasure out of the palace. They swam under the water, but every once in a while, one surfaced to smile at us, her arms full of gold or sapphires or rubies.

Peter, the Lost Boys, and I flew above them, our swords drawn in case the pirates came after Buttercup and the rest of the mermaids. It didn't seem all that likely. As we flew around the island's next bay, I glanced back for one last look at the pirate ship. The torn red sails were still spread all across the deck. The crew was crowded at the helm, where Hook was arguing with Smee really loudly.

"Cap'n, it seems we be out of thread. Noodler used the last of it to sew himself a new shirt."

"Morons, the lot of you," shouted Hook. "How do you expect to repair the sails?"

Giggling, I raced forward to join Peter and the Lost Boys. "We probably don't need to worry about the pirates for a little while."

"Then why do the mermaids have to move?" Dibs grumbled.

Button explained, "It's like with our tree. If the pirates know where it is, it's not safe anymore. We can't know when Hook will come back."

"Then why do we have to help them?" Dibs said, still not convinced.

"We've never helped the mermaids before. I kind of like it," said Kyle.

"And can you think of anything better to do?" Prank asked. The way he said it made me think that the Lost Boys had wanted new adventures for a long while. Peter had disappeared. None of us knew where he'd gone.

In gratitude for our help, Queen Maris sent Buttercup to invite us to a celebration feast at their bay.

"We aren't going to have to eat homemade sushi, are we?" I asked worriedly when we landed and I saw the pile of raw fish and the mound of green-black seaweed that the mermaids had brought us.

Button took matters into his own hands, building a fire to roast the fish and using his sword to chop the seaweed into salad. He hummed while he worked. Apparently, having the Grove of Food Trees hadn't stopped Button from learning how to cook. It smelled wonderful. All our stomachs growled as we waited for him to finish.

Some of the mermaids played tag with a school of flying fish, whose scales glittered in all different colors: silver and gold and magenta and turquoise and emerald.

The mermaids let us watch, but when Prank tried swimming out to join them, they hissed at him and dived down way deep, where we couldn't follow.

Prank looked crestfallen.

"Looks like it's a mermaids-only game," I told him.

"No, I think they still remember the time Prank dipped their combs in ink," Dibs said.

"That was *ages* ago," Prank complained, splashing out of the water.

"Wow, is there *anyone* on the island you haven't annoyed?" I asked.

"The Never trees?" Prank said, grinning sheepishly. We all laughed a little, even Prank.

Something had changed since the fight with the pirates. The Lost Boys had stopped treating me like a guest and started acting like I was one of them. I couldn't get rid of the happy fizzy feeling in my stomach. I walked an inch or two above the ground, hoping that no one would notice how happy I was.

"I wish Tiger Lily and the Cubs had stayed longer," Kyle said, poking at Button's fire with a long stick. "I wanted to talk to Pounce."

"Want to go visit them tomorrow?" I suggested, hoping to see Tiger Lily again.

"Dinner's ready!" Button called proudly from the tall, flat boulder he'd been using as a worktable. Roasted fish sat on six beds of seaweed salad. "Careful with the dishes. We have to give them back."

"Wow. *Sparkly*," Prank said, inspecting the gold plate under his meal.

"I want two fish," said a familiar voice by the edge of the forest beyond the beach. Peter stood there, his fists on his hips. His timing was spooky. Something dangled from a strap in his right hand.

"That's my camera!" I cried, recognizing it.

"Of course it is," Peter said in his cocky way, thrusting it toward Kyle.

"Take a picture of us together," Peter told the littlest Lost Boy, and my mouth was still open with surprise when the camera flashed.

"Wait! Let's get one with *all* of us," I told Kyle. I organized Peter and the Lost Boys in a row, and then I set up the timer on the camera and ran to a spot next to Button. By the time the camera flashed and took the picture, I was smiling like I was supposed to.

Kyle flew over to pick up the camera, and the Lost Boys gathered around him, watching the photos print.

"Can I take some more, Wendy girl?" Kyle said as I handed Peter a plate.

"Sure," I said, taking my plate and walking to the top of a boulder at the water's edge.

The light from Button's fire reflected into the water, and I could see that the mermaids were already enjoying their dinner. Buttercup noticed me and waved enthusiastically, holding a small silver fish with a big bite out of it.

I sat down on the boulder where I could see her. The mermaids' treasure glittered under the water below my feet. Peter sat down next to me in his careless, sprawling way, and the Lost Boys followed, taking seats around me.

My meal was a little weird, now that I saw it up close. The fish still had its eyes, but I forced myself to be brave. I flicked off a few scales and took a bite. "Button, this is delicious! You must be the best chef in Neverland!"

Button smiled widely. "Be careful of the bones," he said with a small shrug.

We all ate together, like one big, Neverland-style family.

The only thing that could have made me happier was if Tink could be there. You know, as long as she wasn't going to yell at me or pull my hair.

The mermaids who had finished their dinner had started to organize the treasure. I watched them as I ate. Gold and silver coins, strings of pearls, loose sapphires and rubies, and assorted dishware that matched the golden plates we were borrowing sparkled in the water.

Then one of the mermaids picked up something that looked familiar, but it was so unexpected—so strange to see in Neverland—that it took me a while to recognize it.

"Hey, it's a cell phone," I said, wondering how it got here. The metallic casing was very shiny—no wonder the mermaids had thought it was treasure.

"What's a cell phone?" Kyle asked.

"It helps you talk to people," I said.

"That's useless," Peter said, laughing. "I'm talking to you right now, aren't I?"

"It helps you talk to people far *away*," I told Peter. The mermaids picked up a laptop, very flat and as shiny as the cell phone. "Oh, look—a computer!"

"I thought Peter banned them from Neverland," Button whispered to Prank.

"A computer? Isn't that what you wanted when you were our mother?" Dibs said, sounding a little hopeful.

I scowled. I really wished he would stop bringing it up.

"She doesn't *have* to be a mother," Kyle said defensively. "She's not a normal Wendy girl."

"Not if she can stop a pirate ship dead in the water," Prank said slyly.

"That's right," Peter said. "We like Ashley just the way she is."

All the Lost Boys raised their eyebrows at the same time. I didn't move or speak.

Peter peered into my face. I shook my hair forward to hide it, but it was too late. "Why are you turning red?" he asked.

"Because you've called me by my name," I whispered back, smiling. Without meaning to, I rose in the air, half a foot above my seat.

Peter grinned.

Suddenly, a head burst through the water.

My first thought was of Neverland's crocodile. I jumped and grabbed Peter's arm, ready to pull us both into the air if I saw any enormous teeth.

20 I Get Crowned Queen

"*I*t's just a mermaid," Peter told me with a half laugh, and I felt kind of sheepish for overreacting.

The mermaid smiled shyly, her wet blue hair plastered to her shoulders. She reached out a webbed hand tentatively and laid a small purple seashell at my feet before swimming to the other side of the bay.

Then another mermaid, a dark-haired one, emerged and dropped a scallop shell in front of me, and then another came, placing a salmon-colored conch shell near my foot.

"I think they're paying tribute," Button said in an

awed voice. All the Lost Boys stared, but Peter crossed his arms and smiled cockily, like he'd expected the mermaids to start a seashell collection for me all along.

One by one, each mermaid gave me a shell until I had a small pile.

Last of all came Queen Maris herself. I gulped.

The mermaid queen had a cold green-eyed stare, long clawlike fingernails, and a smile that revealed all her teeth. She wasn't nearly as friendly as her little sister, and so I was *really* glad that she was on our side.

The mermaid queen smiled wider, looking pleased with herself. I think she enjoyed being a little scary. Even Buttercup—rising out of the water just behind her sister, carrying something folded and golden in her hands—giggled.

Queen Maris raised her hands. All the mermaids in the bay stopped swimming around and became completely still. She said something in a low, ceremonious gurgle.

Buttercup swam forward to translate. "Maris, queen of the mermaids, would like to address Ashley, Wendy girl of the Lost Boys."

I put my plate aside and wiped my hands on my pajamas, hoping that I looked okay.

Queen Maris smiled again and said something else, something much longer. When she finished, all the mermaids started splashing a lot, which was probably their version of applauding.

The rest of us turned to Buttercup, who had a huge smile on her face. "The Wendy girl Ashley has done Queen Maris a great service. First, by rescuing the queen's sister Buttercup—I mean, *me*. Second, by stopping the pirate ship from stealing Queen Maris's treasure. Queen Maris is in the Wendy girl's debt. From this day forward, Queen Maris declares the mermaids allies of the Wendy girl."

Button's mouth hung open, and Dibs rubbed his eyes and looked again, as if he couldn't believe what he was seeing.

"Wow, we've never been allies with the mermaids before," Kyle said.

"Do you think this means they'll stop trying to drown me?" Prank asked.

That's right. Not just friends with the mermaids, but *allies*. Who said it was impossible?

I turned to look at Peter, and the corners of my mouth turned up no matter *how* hard I tried to keep a straight face.

Peter knew exactly what I was thinking. He shrugged, both hands in the air, but his grin was wide and kind of proud.

"I thank you, Queen Maris," I said, trying to be dignified. "I would be honored to be your ally."

After Buttercup translated, the mermaid queen

replied, "We would like to present this token of our appreciation to the Wendy girl."

Buttercup swam toward her sister, grinning broadly and gurgling something quietly. As Queen Maris took the golden cloth from her sister and settled it around my shoulders, Buttercup whispered, "I picked it out myself."

It was a golden coat. It was a little big for me, wet, and very heavy, but the metallic threads shone in the light of the fire. I slid my arms through the sleeves, and a very strange feeling came over me—I stopped worrying about Peter taking me home if I made a mistake or caring so much that Tiger Lily didn't want to be my friend.

With that coat, I felt like I *belonged* in Neverland.

"I think it's my favorite coat ever," I said.

All the mermaids started splashing again, and the Lost Boys got to their feet and cheered. "Ashley! Ashley! Ashley!"

"She's like a queen," Kyle told Dibs over the splashing. "A queen of Neverland."

I ran my hand over the bright, stiff fabric of the coat, liking the idea very much.

"Not bad for her third day here," said Prank.

"If Ashley's the queen, who's the king?" Button asked.

"Peter, of course," said Dibs. "But since he outranks

the Wendy girl, he's more like the emperor."

"Naturally," said Peter, inclining his head with a regal air.

Then I noticed Queen Maris. I didn't think she needed a translation. She was watching us with her chin lowered, beginning to look dangerous again. Even Buttercup looked uneasy, and I knew that the mermaid queen's gratitude could only stretch so far.

"It's only for fun, though," I told her quickly. "We wouldn't give orders or anything."

"Says who?" Peter said, turning to the Lost Boys. *"Bow,"* he demanded.

The Lost Boys all swept him a very fine bow (although Kyle ruined his a little by snorting through his nose).

But the mermaid queen was smiling again, and I knew she understood. She whispered something to Buttercup. My friend dived under the water and emerged a second later with a crown much smaller than the one Queen Maris wore.

This, the mermaid queen took from her sister, and she raised it above her head. Its emeralds and sapphires sparkled in the light of Button's fire. All the mermaids and the Lost Boys fell silent.

She placed the crown on my head. It still dripped, soaking my hair, but I didn't mind. Peter crowed in delight, so I knew it had to look pretty good.

I remembered my manners. "Thank you, Queen Maris."

The mermaid queen inclined her head, looking even more regal than Peter, and then she sank slowly into the water. One by one, the mermaids retreated, following her.

Buttercup was last. I leaned over to say good-bye, and she grabbed the boulder I sat on and pulled herself up to kiss my cheek. "Good night, Ashley."

"Night, Buttercup! See you later!" I said, and my new friend waved and slipped under the water.

"I think we've been dismissed," Dibs said, sounding miffed.

"Lost Boys, prepare to leave!" Peter ordered.

I noticed Prank stuffing a golden plate into his shirt.

"Prank, leave that here!" I said sharply, not wanting to make my new mermaid allies mad by letting one of the Lost Boys steal their dishware.

"Yes, my queen," said Prank sarcastically. I tried to not let it hurt my feelings.

Button took all the plates, scraping them clean and burying the bones in the sand. Kyle grabbed my camera, gathering up the photos he'd taken. Thinking that it would be rude to leave the seashells, I dropped them into my new coat's deep pockets.

"Lost Boys, to bed!" Peter shouted, and Button, Prank, Dibs, and Kyle all launched themselves into the air.

Then Peter turned to me and extended his arm majestically. "Queen Ashley," he said in a grand way, not even the tiniest bit sarcastic.

For this Pretend, I didn't even have to close my eyes. It came so naturally. The crown felt comfortable on my head, as my sword had felt in my hand earlier. I stood a little taller and gazed at the forest around us like it belonged to me, like it would obey all my commands.

My fingers and toes tingling, I took Peter's hand and smiled. When we flew through the trees to catch up with the Lost Boys, my new coat fluttered in the breeze and threw little bits of light on the leaves around us.

"Two presents!" I said to myself. "It's like Christmas came early."

"What's Christmas?" Button asked.

"You don't know what Christmas is?" I said, aghast.

"I remember Christmas!" Kyle said happily. "There's this tree, you see, with these presents wrapped up under it. On Christmas morning, you get to open them."

"Presents?" said Button with sleepy enthusiasm.

"We should have Christmas morning right now!" Dibs said.

"No, not yet," I said, starting to feel excited. Maybe back home, Christmas hadn't worked out the way I wanted, but in Neverland, Christmas could be exactly what I Pretended it to be.

All the Lost Boys turned to me, shocked.

"You don't like presents?" Kyle said.

"Not when she already got hers," Dibs said. He pointed at my new coat and crown. He was probably going to be annoyed with me until the end of time. Now that I was queen, I decided to ignore this. I would rise above it.

"Of *course* I like presents. But one of the best parts of Christmas is getting everything ready, don't you think, Your Imperial Majesty?" I asked, appealing to Emperor Peter.

"I decree that Christmas shall be in two days," he replied in his most emperorlike voice.

"*Decree*—that's very regal word," Dibs said, turning to me with a look that clearly said he blamed me for Peter's new flavor of bossiness.

"Neverland's first Christmas," Kyle said dreamily. "But why didn't we have it before?"

"Because we didn't have Ashley here before," Button said.

"Yeah—why didn't you bring her earlier, Peter?" Prank asked, grinning at me. "Now we have mermaids for allies and Christmas in two days."

"Ha!" I said, thinking that he was being sarcastic.

"I'm serious," Prank said, sounding wounded. "This Wendy girl has got to be the best thing to happen to

Neverland since Pan himself."

I half grinned at the compliment—at least, until Peter shifted beside me. He wasn't frowning exactly, but he had a faraway look with a little line between his eyebrows, like he was thinking about something he didn't like very much. I was about to tell him that Prank didn't mean it, but then Peter caught me looking.

He grinned, confident as ever.

Maybe there wasn't anything to worry about, after all.

I smiled back, my mind filling with Christmas plans. "Who wants a story before bed?"

21 I Catch a Little Lightning

That night, for the Lost Boys' bedtime story, I recited "The Night Before Christmas" from memory. When I couldn't remember the details, I made some up. I figured that they probably wouldn't know the difference, but apparently the Lost Boys had gotten a few of their Christmas memories back.

Halfway through, Prank said suspiciously, "I don't remember Rudolph the Red-nosed Reindeer making a gingerbread house out of mini marshmallows and gumdrops."

"Or Santa installing a hot chocolate machine in the kitchen," said Kyle, and I squirmed uncomfortably, wondering if I could convince them that Santa's elves rewrote the story recently.

"Maybe my mom skipped that part when she read it to me," Dibs murmured sleepily.

"I think we're getting Ashley's new and improved version," Button said from the branch where he was rigging up a new hammock for me, but he said it fondly. All the Lost Boys smiled.

A gust of wind whistled through the leaves. The branches around us tossed and pitched.

I drew my golden coat tighter around me, hunching up against the unexpected cold. A huge raindrop landed on my shoulder, splashing my neck.

"Storm's coming," Peter said, his eyes glittering. He said it like the storm was an enemy he was eager to fight.

The rain came harder, striking the ground with sharp plops, and I knew it was about to pour.

Peter didn't seem worried. He just flew up and up, higher than the tallest tree, and crowed at the sky, like he was challenging it.

I wasn't finished with the story, and I didn't want to go to bed just yet. I looked around for a covered area where we could all fit. "Lost Boys! Under Peter's house!" I ordered.

"You know, since you got crowned queen, you've started to be as bossy as Peter," Prank said offhandedly as we rose in the air.

"What? You normally sit out in the open and get soaked during every thunderstorm?" I pointed out, feeling more raindrops. "It's for your own good."

"Mothers say that too," said Dibs with a small smile.

"Do you want me to finish the story or not?" I said, hands on my hips.

Dibs, Kyle, and Prank zipped up and dived under Peter's house, settling in the branches there, eager to hear the end. But not Button.

As the rain fell faster, he made straight for the staircase, pulling back the leaves that covered his carvings and sketches. "Oh no!" he murmured, and with a pang of sympathy, I knew that the rain had washed away the charcoal drawings, the ones he hadn't gotten a chance to carve yet.

White chunks of ice joined the rain and thunked against the ground. The hailstones stung where they hit my shoulder, even through my new coat. It had to be even worse for the Lost Boys.

"Button!" I called worriedly. "Come on."

Defeated, Button climbed up to us and dropped heavily to a seat, head bent.

He looked so sad, blinking hard at the branch right below him.

"I'm sorry about your drawings, Button," I said softly, and he just shrugged, Peter-like, as if it didn't matter to him.

"What drawings?" Dibs said curiously, which I took

as a good reason to change the subject.

"Where was I?" I asked brightly.

"Donner was snacking on the gingerbread house," said Kyle excitedly.

Then I launched straight into the part where Prancer and Blitzen started arguing over the last candy cane so loudly that it woke the children up.

"Merry Christmas to all, and to all a good night!" I finished, three minutes later.

The Lost Boys all clapped, even Dibs.

"I think I like this version better," Prank whispered to Kyle, and then thunder rumbled in the distance, making us all jump.

Peter landed on the branch next to me, his feet slapping against the bark. "It's time for an adventure."

"Now?" I asked skeptically. I mean, it *was* raining. Besides, I *had* just finished a bedtime story. That usually meant it was time for bed.

"A storm's the best time for this," Peter said mischievously, and he jumped from the branch and glided away. "Come on."

"Lightning?" Dibs asked excitedly, jumping into the air.

Prank grinned. "What else?"

I remembered the fairies. "You mean, lightning *catching*?" I asked, flying behind the Lost Boys.

"We'll show you," Button said as Kyle grabbed my

hand, tugging me faster.

Then Peter zipped through the trees, and we flew after him. Thunder cracked again, closer this time.

I was the only one who jumped. "Is it safe to be in the forest? I mean, at home, lightning can kill people."

"Scared of a little storm, Wendy girl?" Prank teased.

"Hey, if I can handle a few pirates, then I can definitely handle a little thunder," I replied hotly, but I still looked up just in case a bolt surprised us on the way.

"Don't worry. They try never to fall this far inland," Button explained.

That made me curious. The Lost Boys talked like the lightning bolts were living people.

In the dark, you couldn't really see the forest. The trees just seemed like huge crooked shapes, trunks and limbs we swerved to avoid. The air was full of the sound of raindrops plopping on leaves and the wind whistling through the branches.

Then the trees ended suddenly, and we came to the shore. Waves crashed at the base of the cliff we stood on, throwing up water so high that I tasted salt on my lips.

The Lost Boys all turned to see my reaction, but it took me a moment to realize what I was looking at.

Hundreds of lights—purplish, white, and blue— swarmed over the ocean's surface, darting this way and that, like they were searching for something. Even over the sound of the waves and the storm, I heard their anxious chimes.

"But I don't see any lightning," I said.

With one of his pleased smirks, Peter pointed at the sky.

Gray clouds sat on the horizon, lit by the lightning that crackled within. Then, one bolt broke free. Instead of appearing all at once like a jagged glowing line, this lightning fell slowly. It meandered from point to point, leaving a trail behind it like a comet, cutting the sky in half.

The fairies zoomed across the water toward it, but too late. With a merry twinkle, the lightning dived into the sea and winked out.

"And . . . safe," Prank said, like an umpire at a baseball game, half grinning.

When the thunder reached us, it sounded suspiciously like a chuckle.

Disappointed, the fairies gathered together in one big swarm of lights, searching the sky again.

Something about the way the lightning had twinkled seemed very familiar, almost like I had seen it before someplace else. "The lightning bolts," I said excitedly, "they're not falling stars, are they?"

Peter laughed, delighted. "Of course they are. I knew you were a smart Wendy girl."

We watched another star fall, hopping down the

sky from point to point, creating a trail of lightning behind it.

"At home, my teachers say that lightning is electricity, caused when molecules in storm clouds rub together," I murmured.

"Grown-ups," Peter said scornfully. "They don't know anything."

Then Button added, very quickly, "But lightning *is* dangerous where you come from. The stars get angry, because they can't fall the way they want to, like they can in Neverland."

"I wish they could," I whispered as another star wiggled down the sky and the fairies rushed toward it. "They're beautiful."

Peter stepped off the cliff, hovering in the air across from me. "Want to catch one?"

"Do they really give you a wish?" I asked excitedly.

"Duh," said Dibs. "That's why we're here."

"Anything you want!" Kyle cried, squeezing my hand harder in anticipation.

"You know what they say about wishing on falling stars," said Prank.

"But I caught a star on the way over here," I pointed out. "A bunch of times."

Dibs rolled his eyes. "*Falling* was the operative word there. You can't expect any wishes if the star is still in the sky."

Then Peter grabbed my other hand, dragging Kyle

and me over the water. We went so fast that I could hear Kyle giggling with delight.

The fairies guessed what we were up to, and they didn't want to share. When we flew close, they reached out to grab our clothes, our hair, our toes; but Prank and Button cut them off. Laughing, Peter twisted out of the fairies' reach, taking Kyle and me with him.

I laughed too, looking back. For a second, I thought I saw Tinker Bell, but when Peter swerved again, I lost sight of her.

"There!" Kyle shouted, pointing.

Another star emerged from the storm clouds, cartwheeling down to the ocean. Peter flew faster, tugging us along with him.

Maybe Peter could predict where the star was headed. Maybe the star recognized Peter and arched our way. But the star fell straight toward us.

Peter's hand stretched out. I thought he would catch it, but at the last second, he pulled me in front of him and let go of my hand.

The star fell into my palm instead. It buzzed a little, warm and pleasant, and I felt it over my whole body, like leaning against a dryer. For a minute, I could only stare.

"Well?" Peter said eagerly.

"Make a wish," Kyle said, letting go of my hand so that I could cup the star between both palms.

Over his shoulder, I saw Prank, Button, and even Dibs grinning widely—as happy as they would've been if they had caught the star themselves.

"Go on," urged Peter.

In my hand, the star wiggled impatiently, like it agreed with him.

I could've wished that Tiger Lily would like me, or Tink, but after everything that had happened that day, making that change didn't feel so important. Actually, I wanted just one more thing from my trip to Neverland: not to get in trouble when I went home.

The star glowed a little brighter, its rays shooting past my fingers. It had heard me.

"Now let it go," Peter said.

I kissed the star good-bye—the buzzing tickled my teeth—and then I opened my hands. The star dived into the water with a fizzing sound and swam out of sight.

When I looked up, Peter and the Lost Boys beamed at me so widely that I wondered what exactly they thought I'd wished for.

22
The Never Birds Donate Feathers

$\mathcal{I}$ had never been in charge of a Christmas celebration before. It had a weird effect on me. Making plans this time, I wanted to make it special *for other people.*

As soon as I woke up the next morning, I grabbed my backpack and flew into the forest, far enough away from the Tree Home that the others couldn't see me. I searched the front pocket of my bag and found what I'd been looking for—a small Baggie full of cookies, candy canes, and chocolate. My teacher had handed them out before she dismissed class a few days before.

The trip to Neverland had clearly been kind of rough.

The contents had broken into bits. Only crumbs were left.

I smiled. That actually helped me.

With a sharp stick, I dug a hole in the ground and poured the crumbs inside. Then I patted dirt over them and Pretended as hard as I could: it would sprout sometime before night fell, a food tree with a Christmas tree shape. Instead of ornaments, it would have gingerbread cookies, candy canes, and other treats.

My fingers and toes tingled a little, and I knew that it had worked.

After breakfast, I decided that as the youngest Lost Boy, Kyle should pick out the Christmas tree. Dibs was the only one who protested, and I told him not to spoil it for Kyle or I would tell Santa not to bring him any presents. That was what Mom always told me around Christmas to make sure I obeyed her. Dibs put Hook's hat back on to make himself feel better.

Kyle chose a ten-foot-tall fir about thirty paces from the Tree Home. The actual decorating slowed us down a little, because we had to *make* all of the decorations. It took a while for the Lost Boys to understand how it worked.

Prank, for example, took the red-and-beige seashell I handed him and threw it at the Christmas tree. When the shell bounced down through the branches and landed on the forest floor, he said, "Ashley, I think this ornament's broken."

I couldn't answer at first. I was laughing too hard.

"What about this?" Button said, raising the conch shell I had given him a moment before. He had wrapped a slender vine around and around the middle of the shell and knotted the excess vine to make a loop.

"Exactly!" I said, and Kyle clapped happily.

Peter flew closer and inspected the ornament carefully. "I decree that this is the very first Christmas ornament in Neverland."

"Put it on the tree," I ordered.

Button smiled bashfully as he found a branch he liked and placed Neverland's first ever ornament on Neverland's first ever Christmas tree.

"Do you think Santa knows how to get to Neverland?" Kyle asked me.

"I don't know," I said, a little surprised at the question.

"He might not know to come—because we're celebrating Christmas on a different day than other people," Button said hesitantly, and then all the Lost Boys looked a little worried.

I hadn't thought about it before. But I couldn't imagine a Christmas without presents. If no one else was bringing them, that just meant I had to take matters into my own hands.

Flying off as sneakily as I could, I started gathering materials. I would have to make some gifts, but I had brought most of them with me in my backpack.

The problem was that there was nowhere to *wrap* the presents. Someone turned up everywhere I tried to hide. When I hid behind an oak tree at the edge of the clearing, Button came, searching the ground for new acorns he could use for the garland. When I hunched down in my hammock, Prank came up to get a bunch of gray and light-green feathers out of his hiding place—the foot-long ones he had yanked from the Never birds' tails months before.

Finally, I slipped into Peter's house, feeling a little guilty. I was pretty sure I wasn't allowed in there uninvited, but I was kind of desperate. I tried to hurry—to keep from getting caught.

Sitting on the floor between the window and the bed, I pulled the Lost Boys' presents out of my backpack and wrapped them first. At home, I would've had wrapping paper and ribbons, but I made do with flexible leaves and bits of vine.

While I was at it, I went ahead and made the presents I'd planned. I took all the seashells that were too small to make good tree ornaments and used a very skinny vine to string them together. Maybe it wasn't the most artistic necklace in the world, but Neverland seashells are so bright and colorful that it looked pretty anyway. As I wrapped it, I was sure Mom would like it. Maybe she would even like it so much that she would rethink grounding me for accidentally feeding her iPod to the Neverland crocodile.

I knew exactly what I would give Dad, too. Other people might think that nobody would ever like to get a bunch of leaves for Christmas, but my dad taught botany. He *loved* stuff like that. Actually, if he found out that I went to Neverland *without* bringing back leaf samples, he might be *more* likely to punish me.

The last present was almost impossible. What could I possibly give to Peter Pan? I mean, he had kind of given me a falling star the night before. It was hard to compete with that.

Finally, after thinking for a long time and flipping through the Polaroids in my backpack, I had an idea. I just didn't know if I would be brave enough to give it to him. I pulled aside four sticks and started to tie them together, but then the door creaked open.

It was Peter, staring at me.

I shoved all the wrapped gifts into my backpack and out of sight, and then I turned guiltily to the doorway, not sure if I could talk myself out of this one. "Hey, it's not like you didn't show up in *my* room uninvited a few days ago when you came to take me to Neverland. I was just working on the presents."

Then I waited for him to tell me that no Lost Boy or Wendy girl was allowed in his house without permission.

But he just laughed, opening the door wider. "I guess we're even then. Come on—the Lost Boys want you to check the Christmas tree and see if they've decorated it right."

I was kind of shocked that he handled it so calmly, but I wasn't about to question it. Not getting in trouble was definitely a happy thought.

I glided across the room and through the doorway, smiling quickly at Peter before flying down. Prank, Button, and Dibs had set up a workstation next to the Christmas tree—a red blanket over the grass, with piles of acorns and feathers.

"Are there any other kinds of decorations?" Button asked, looking up from the acorns he was linking together. "It's just ornaments and garland and the star on top?"

I examined the tree carefully. I didn't know what kind of tree I would end up having when I got back home. I wanted this one to be perfect. "Usually, there are lights, too."

Prank passed me a new feather ornament he'd just made, and I held it up, admiring the way it looked almost silver in the sunlight.

"Too bad we can't convince some fairies that this is

a great place to sleep," Prank said, looking thoughtful. "Tink might be able to do it—"

"Tink is banished," Peter reminded us all in a thunderous voice. It was true. We hadn't seen even a fairy glimmer all morning. Then, softening a little, he added, "At least until after Christmas."

"There aren't very many left," Dibs complained, poking through the broken and bent feathers.

There was a flutter of wings on the far side of the clearing. A dozen Never birds burst through the leaves and sailed over to us.

Prank's eyes widened nervously. "You don't think they want their feathers back, do you?" he whispered.

I hid the new feather ornament behind me as the Never birds landed in a semicircle around us, eyeing me with dark beady eyes. Spot clucked hello. As we watched, their feathers lost the gray and green of the Never trees and started to look more and more like the red blanket on the forest floor.

"If you challenge Ashley, you challenge Pan," said Peter loyally, drawing his sword. I thought it was very noble of him, but I put a hand on his arm to make sure he didn't overreact like he had during the muffin incident.

But the Never birds just spread their wings and bent so low that their beaks almost brushed the ground.

"Did they just *bow*?" asked Dibs incredulously,

peering at them from under Hook's hat.

"Maybe they heard that you were the queen of Neverland," Prank said, half joking, but Spot nodded eagerly.

"They came to pay their respects," Peter said, sounding smug, like he'd arranged the whole thing.

"But it's just *Pretend*," I whispered back.

"Where's Kyle?" Prank asked as the Never birds straightened back up. "He would *love* this."

"He went to go see the mermaids," Dibs said. "He wanted to get a starfish or a sand dollar for the top of the tree."

"I'll get him," Button said, and I heard the leaves rustle as he flew toward the mermaids' new home.

The Never birds all turned around abruptly. At first, I thought they were going to fly off, but then they all reached back, took the longest and fluffiest of their own tail feathers in their beaks, and yanked.

The Lost Boys stared.

In a tidy line, the Never birds waddled over to me. When Spot stopped and made a sort of honking noise, I stretched out my hands, palms up. One by one, the birds deposited the tail feathers into them.

"Not fair," Prank muttered.

"Thank you," I said, admiring the feathers. They were as red as the blanket the Never birds had been standing on.

The Never birds all turned around again, and each grasped another tail feather in its beak.

"No!" I cried, and the Never birds looked up at me with their beady eyes. "No, thank you, but you don't have to. If you give me too many, you might affect your ability to fly."

The Never birds turned to each other with excited little trills, as if they were discussing a new development.

"What did I do?" I asked as Spot began to rub her head against my leg, like a cat.

"You proved yourself a wise and judicious ruler," Prank said, half joking again, and three of the Never birds nodded, trilling happily.

They weren't the only ones to hear about me being crowned queen.

The lion arrived just three minutes later, before Button and Kyle came back.

One minute, Prank and I were putting up the string of acorns that Button had made, and the next, all the Lost Boys were up in the air, shouting at the top of their lungs.

I understood what Dibs was saying first. "Lions! Lions!"

Still on the ground, Peter and I turned at the same time. A lion stalked into the clearing. He shook his mane and blinked at me with big, topaz eyes.

I gulped and stopped myself from taking a step back. "I didn't know that there were lions in Neverland."

"Yep, lions. And tigers," Prank said, starting to count on his fingers again. "And bears."

"Wolves, too," Peter added.

"They *can* eat you," Dibs said sharply.

With sleepy, half-closed eyes, the lion started to walk slowly across the clearing, lashing his tail.

I looked at Peter, who didn't move. I decided that if Peter wasn't afraid, then I wasn't going to be either. We would make a united front as queen and emperor of Neverland—for the Lost Boys' sake.

"He doesn't seem hungry," I said, trying to reassure myself.

He really didn't. He came up very close, so close that I could feel his hot breath on my face.

Peter smiled at me, the smile that carried a hint of pride. "He heard that you were the queen of Neverland too."

The lion yowled in agreement.

Suddenly, I wondered if my ability to Pretend was a little too strong for my own good.

But really, I didn't mind it all that much. My fingers and toes tingled. Pretending to be Queen Ashley, Lion Tamer, had its perks.

I stretched out an arm toward the lion slowly, ready to fly up and join the Lost Boys if he attacked. But the big cat just thrust his head into my hand and began to purr. His mane was incredibly soft.

"Aww, I think he likes me," I said.

When I offered him my other hand, he licked it. His tongue was so scratchy it tickled, but I didn't giggle. Laughing might hurt his feelings.

Peter put his hands on his fists, looking on smugly.

"Whoa," Dibs said, impressed.

"Kyle *really* has to come back," Prank said.

The lion leaned forward suddenly. Dibs and Prank shouted, worried that the cat was getting ready to pounce, but he just knelt, looking at me expectantly. I had a pretty good idea what he wanted.

I flew up a little and landed gingerly on his back. The lion roared with delight and took off at a run. I had to grab his mane to keep from falling off.

"Not so fast," I said, steering him back to the Lost Boys.

"You're riding a *lion*," said Prank, as if it was a trick he had always wanted to try.

I shrugged. "I saw it in a movie once."

"Kyle *has* to see this," said Dibs, and Prank nodded.

"He—," said someone on the other side of the clearing. We all turned. Button stood on the ground, grasping a tree for support, as if he couldn't think of a thought happy enough to get him into the air.

His face was white. "Kyle's been captured!"

23
Tiger Lily's Little Brother Complains about His Sister

"*P*irates!" Peter cried automatically, drawing his sword.

But Button shook his head. "The mermaids say that it was Tiger Lily's tribe."

A knot formed in my stomach. What could Kyle have possibly done to upset the princess?

Peter lowered his sword a little, puzzled. "The Cubs?"

"But they've always been friendly," Dibs said, frowning.

"Well, since Peter saved Tiger Lily from drowning, anyway," Prank said.

To me, Button added, "When the first Wendy was here."

"Maybe it's just a misunderstanding," I said, stroking the lion's mane.

"I don't think so," Button said. "The mermaids said that Kyle got caught in a trap right by the shore, and while they were trying to figure out a way to free him, Tiger Lily and a few braves came and took him away."

"Maybe they thought it was me," Prank said softly, sounding nervous. "I kind of did something. The day before Ashley got here. With some water balloons, and their hunting practice . . ."

Peter and I exchanged a look. We were both trying to stay calm for the younger kids. Okay, so maybe that was just me.

"I know I haven't been here long," I said slowly, "but I'm sure that Tiger Lily can tell the difference between you and Kyle. Let's go pay her a visit."

"We can't," Dibs said.

"They moved their camp after that trick," Prank said apologetically.

"You don't know where they are?" I asked, starting to get even *more* worried about Kyle.

"Tink would," Peter said, raising his hand to his mouth to whistle for her.

But then the lion roared, making all the Lost Boys jump.

Button took flight, translating for the big cat. "He

says that he knows where the Cubs are camping."

"That's very helpful," I told the lion. "Would you please take us there? Quietly though—I don't want them to know that we've come, at least at first."

The lion yowled and bounded into the woods. I bent forward and clung to his mane, glancing behind me to make sure the others were following.

Peter burst through the leaves just above me, looking grim and determined. His golden blade glinted. Prank and Button flew just behind me and the lion, and Dibs appeared in the air to my left, holding Hook's hat to make sure it didn't blow off.

I knew that we were all thinking the same thing: if Tiger Lily had done anything to hurt Kyle, she wouldn't find us so friendly after all.

We found the Cubs' camp at the opposite end of the island, just beside the cliff where the fairies' tree grew. The lion stalked forward noiselessly. When we were close enough, I tugged lightly on his mane. He stopped, and Peter and the Lost Boys landed on branches around us. There were only a few trees between us and the clearing.

At first, it didn't seem like anything strange was going on—except maybe that the tribe acted much more serious than they had been at the Grove of Food Trees. The Cubs lined the cliff's edge, staring out over the water. Tiger Lily stood a little apart and above, the beaded feathers in her hair whipping back and forth in the wind. She looked beautiful and fierce.

I was having a hard time remembering why I ever wanted to be her friend.

"I don't see Kyle," Dibs said.

Peter leaned forward, hanging from a slender tree's trunk. He was angrier than I had ever seen him. "The pole."

Two Cubs held both ends of a long, wooden pole. Kyle hung from the middle of it, bound with rope. He wasn't crying or anything, determined to be brave; but he looked out over the water too, as still and as white as he had been when Prank told him that Never birds ate Lost Boys named Kyle.

"They're not going to throw him off," Prank said uncertainly. "Are they, Peter?"

"No," said Peter fiercely.

"Not if I have anything to do with it," I added.

The lion under me started to growl, warning us.

One of the braves—the shortest one closest to Tiger Lily—had turned away from the ocean toward us.

I opened my mouth to lead the charge, but Button whispered, "It's okay, Ashley."

"We still have *one* friend among the Cubs," Peter said.

The brave walked into the trees, holding his head

high and his back very straight. Then I recognized the red stripes painted down his bare arms. It was Pounce. When he reached us, he took in the presence of Peter and the Lost Boys without batting an eye, but when he saw my new lion friend, his eyes bugged out a little.

"Pouncing Squirrel," Peter said, inclining his head in his new regal way.

"My sister has lost her mind," said Pounce, sounding a lot like a really frustrated younger brother. "I come to you in the hope that you will stop her from doing something that all of us shall regret."

"So, she did capture Kyle on purpose," said Button sadly.

Pounce shook his head. "She wanted to capture the Wendy girl."

"Me?" I said, shocked. "What did I ever do to her? Is she still mad about the thing with the pirates and the cupcakes?"

"She saw you cut the sails of the *Jolly Roger.* You are a warrior, as no Wendy girl has been before," Pounce said. "And my sister also heard that you have been named Neverland's queen."

The knot in my stomach got a little bigger.

I'd been so proud of myself yesterday, especially when the mermaids named us allies. It never occurred to me that someone wouldn't like me changing things in Neverland.

"That was just *Pretend*," I whispered.

"The great cat you tamed does not think so," said Pounce, pointing at the lion I was riding.

"How did you hear about Ashley being queen?" Button asked.

"A mermaid told a dolphin, who told a flamingo, who told a Never bird, who told a squirrel, who told me," said Pounce. That made me think that *Pouncing Squirrel* might not be such a lame name after all.

At the top of the cliff, Tiger Lily let out a high-pitched, triumphant yell, and the braves echoed her halfheartedly.

Pounce jumped. "We don't have much time. They have spotted him already."

"Who?" Button asked.

"My sister is proud," Pounce told us, looking pained. "She promised Croc that she would feed him today with human blood, and so she will feed him." He turned to me. "Even if she does not have the human she wanted."

"But Kyle can still fly, right?" I said hopefully, turning to Peter. "Even if they throw him off the cliff?"

"If he still has fairy dust," Prank said.

"If he can think of a happy thought after seeing all those teeth," Dibs added.

Pounce looked at Peter. "The tribe does not wish to fight the Lost Boys. If you attempt to rescue Kyle, we will not stop you. But if you attack our princess, we will be forced to protect her. Do you understand?"

A noise filled the air, even louder than the waves crashing below.

"What's that sound?" Dibs asked, wide-eyed.

"Christmas bells," I said automatically. Gulping, I turned back to the cliff.

At the edge, the two braves holding Kyle raised the pole over their heads. Kyle squirmed, trying to twist free. They let go. Kyle fell out of sight.

"No!" I shouted, and the lion under me sprang forward.

24
We Snatch Kyle from the Jaws of Death

*A*ll the braves turned to look. Tiger Lily gave another yell, a battle cry. My lion answered her with a roar. The braves leaped out of the way.

The lion stopped at the cliff's edge, and I dived off his back.

For once, I didn't have a plan. I was *way* too worried to have a plan.

Kyle was already halfway down, going so fast that the pole whistled. The crocodile swam directly under him, its tail lashing through the sea foam.

I flew faster.

The crocodile opened its jaws.

" . . . bells, jingle bells," went the familiar song.

I stretched out both hands, reaching out for the end of the pole that Kyle was tied to.

"Ashley!" he cried.

My hands closed around the wood, and I held on tight. For a minute, we hovered in midair, staring at each other and breathing hard. My arms started to feel the strain. Kyle gulped and looked down.

We were only fifteen feet from the water. I could hear the music even better now: "Oh, what fun it is to ride in a one-horse open sleigh. Hey!"

The crocodile snapped its yellow teeth.

"That was really close," Kyle said.

"We're not out of this yet," I reminded him. My muscles started to tremble, and I gripped the pole with both hands until my knuckles turned white. I *refused* to drop him. "You're really heavy."

I flew upward with the happiest thought I could muster (*Kyle's alive—I saved him*), but we only went up an inch. With the added weight of the pole and all the rope, Kyle was just too heavy for me.

On top of that, the coat that the mermaids had given me kept getting caught in the shore's high winds, blowing me off course.

"Bows!" said Tiger Lily's cold voice. "Take aim!"

"Uh-oh," murmured Kyle.

Along the cliff's edge, the braves lifted their bows,

drawing arrows slowly and reluctantly from quivers on their back. I had nowhere to go. We were as trapped as Buttercup had been in the pirates' net the day before.

"Not fair!" I shouted, glaring at Tiger Lily. There wasn't much else I could do this time. I couldn't even talk my way out of it.

My lion roared and swatted, knocking two bows over the cliff's edge, but then the braves loosed some arrows at him. He bounded into the woods—out of the fight.

The crocodile snapped its jaws again, eager for a meal. "Jingle all the way."

The princess only looked smug. Then something green and gold flashed over her head, and her expression changed.

A second later, another pair of hands grabbed the other end of Kyle's pole. With the weight so much lighter, my arms stopped trembling. I breathed a sigh of relief.

"You should've waited for me," Peter told me sharply.

"If I had waited one more second, Kyle would be reptile food," I snapped. Maybe I was a little testier than usual. It had been a *very* close call.

"Yeah," Kyle said, nodding so hard that the pole wobbled. "That would be bad. Could we please move a little farther away?"

Peter and I exchanged a look and started flying slowly upward. The crocodile lashed its tail, throwing up spray.

"Bye, crocodile!" Kyle called, giggling madly.

"I think he's in shock," I told Peter.

The sound of sleigh bells filled the air again. The song had started over.

"Ashley, the crocodile is singing," Kyle said. "Why is it singing?"

"It swallowed my iPod," I said absently, thinking about the Cubs. "Mom's probably going to ground me when I go home."

The other side of the pole dipped. I looked toward Peter in alarm, worried that someone had shot at him. But Peter was fine. He was just looking at me with a strange expression.

Kyle began singing along with the crocodile. "Dashing through the snow, in a one-horse open sleigh."

"When you go home?" Peter repeated.

He sounded stunned, and I couldn't figure out why. A few days ago, he couldn't stop thinking up excuses to send me there.

"I have to go back," I reminded him. "It's almost Christmas."

I couldn't remember exactly when Christmas—the real Christmas—was. It was strange that I couldn't remember, but I knew that it had to be close.

"O'er the fields we go," sang Kyle, "laughing all the way."

We had flown up above the edge of the cliff. Tiger Lily scowled, her dark eyes narrowed. Beyond the line of braves, Pounce stood with Dibs, Prank, and Button, arms folded over his chest like he was in charge. It took me a second to figure out what he was doing, but then I realized: the Cubs couldn't shoot at the Lost Boys if Tiger Lily's brother was standing right next to them.

For a long moment, Peter and Tiger Lily stared at each other, looking murderous. It was a stalemate.

Then the brave closest to Tiger Lily turned to her. "Princess, Pan has been a great ally to our people, and the lion tamer is a great warrior," he said. "This fight can be avoided."

"Who's the lion tamer?" Kyle whispered to Button.

"Ashley," Button whispered back.

I straightened up and raised my chin like I thought a warrior should.

"Wow. I can't believe I missed that. Ashley, can you tame one again so I can see?" Kyle didn't know that we were still in danger.

Then I realized I had forgotten to bring any weapons. Some great warrior.

"Give me your sword," I asked Peter. "I have to cut Kyle free."

Peter passed it over wordlessly, without looking away from the princess, but Tiger Lily turned to me with a sudden smile.

"I see," she said. "The Lost Boys have a new chieftain."

I scowled at her and sliced through the ropes holding Kyle. "Well, that's the stupidest thing I've heard all day."

Peter obviously didn't think so. He snatched his sword back with a ferocious scowl, a sure sign that he took her comment as a grievous insult.

I wasn't too worried at first. Peter took a lot of things as an insult. I was too busy making sure that Kyle was okay.

"Can we go back now?" I asked Peter, hoping to leave before Tiger Lily forced Pounce back to her side and somebody accidentally loosed an arrow. "We have a Christmas tree to finish decorating."

"She gives many orders," Tiger Lily said, her smile openly mocking. "Even to the great Peter Pan."

I rolled my eyes. "Peter, she's just trying to make you mad on *purpose*—"

"Quiet!" Peter interrupted.

I pressed my lips together, watching carefully. I was kind of hoping that Peter wasn't as angry as he seemed—that he was just putting on a show for Tiger Lily and her Cubs.

Tiger Lily smiled wider.

That settled it. I never wanted to see that particular princess again. After what she'd almost done to Kyle, I would rather make friends with Hook than Tiger Lily.

"We're leaving," Peter said shortly. When he rose into the air, Button, Prank, and Dibs followed, still sticking close to Pounce, who dashed into the woods with them.

"If you ever try to harm one of us again, I won't be so lenient," Peter said, heading into the trees.

At that statement, the braves started to look a little nervous, and even Tiger Lily's feet shifted uncomfortably. I took Kyle's hand and jumped up into the air, sticking my tongue out at the princess as we went.

25
Peter Acts Like an Emperor

*O*nce the leaves closed behind us, I hugged Kyle tightly. "I was so *worried* about you."

"*Ashley*, I'm not a kid," Kyle complained, with the same fierce expression he used every time someone called him little, but I could tell he liked the attention.

In the woods, Pounce and the Lost Boys clapped each other on the back, smiling widely as Kyle and I arrived. Everyone except Peter, who narrowed his eyes when he saw me.

"Thanks, Pounce," Kyle said.

Pounce grinned. "Someone had to do something

about my mad sister. But you should not linger. The woods are unsafe. Pirates still search for Hook's hat."

Dibs grabbed the brim with both hands protectively.

"Are *you* going to be okay?" Button asked Pounce. "Tiger Lily—"

"The others won't listen to her for a while," Pounce said with a shrug before speeding off through the trees, *away* from the Cubs' camp. (I had the feeling he didn't want to face his sister until after she cooled off a little.) Running, he turned back once and waved good-bye.

Now that the adventure was over, the Lost Boys started to celebrate, whooping loudly.

Peter didn't join them. He just took off wordlessly, flying toward the Tree Home. I rushed to catch up.

"We saved him!" I told Peter, hoping that he would crow.

He ignored me. He'd never ignored me before. Called me stupid, yes. Threatened to take me home, several times. But not this.

It didn't make sense. A few hours earlier, he'd been treating me like a friend—an equal. He hadn't even gotten mad at me for sneaking into his house.

The Lost Boys hadn't noticed Peter's bad mood. Flying behind me, Kyle was teaching the rest of them all the Christmas carols he remembered. Dibs kept getting the lyrics wrong, singing "Rudolph, the Rough-nosed Reindeer."

"Peter, what's wrong?" I asked, but he still didn't say anything. "Peter?"

He wouldn't even look at me.

It had to be what Tiger Lily said.

I *knew* it wasn't true. Even the idea that I could be the Lost Boys' leader seemed ridiculous. I mean, Peter was a legend. I was just a visitor.

But I didn't know how to tell Peter without upsetting him more.

When we came to the clearing with the Tree Home, he didn't even land with us. He stood in the air, his fists on his hips, his back to me.

He wasn't being fair, but I didn't know how to make him feel better.

"Okay, Lost Boys," I said, pretending to be cheerful. "Time to finish decorating!"

Kyle stopped singing "O Christmas Tree" in midnote. "I never got a starfish from the mermaids," he said, looking worried. "Not even a sand dollar."

"You are *not* going back," I said sharply, the thought filling me with horror. "Not with a crazy princess on the loose."

"She was after you, Ashley," Dibs said. "She'll get over it."

"Maybe we could *make* a star for the top of the tree," Button suggested.

"But I *wanted* to see the mermaids," Kyle said sadly.

"Well, maybe we'll go visit them later," I said doubtfully. "But if we do, nobody goes out alone. And we need to figure out a way to signal each other if we run into tr—"

"Stop!" Peter shouted fiercely.

We all looked up at him in surprise. His gaze met mine immediately, and when I realized he was talking to me, I held very still, afraid of him for the first time.

"I don't want to decorate the Christmas tree," Peter announced.

"Okay," I said cautiously.

All the Lost Boys drooped their shoulders a little bit, disappointed.

Peter didn't notice. He twirled his golden sword with an expert flourish. "It is time for a splendid adventure."

I frowned. It wasn't a *good* time. It didn't look like Kyle had recovered from the last adventure, and the sun would set in a couple of hours. But Peter was in no mood for an argument.

"Fine, just let me get my sword," I said, flying up to the trunk of the Tree Home to Kyle's hiding place where I'd left it. "What kind of warrior would I be if—"

"No," Peter said. He said it quietly, but he sounded

so angry and so triumphant at the same time that I turned to stare at him. "You're staying here," he told me. "You all are. I will go alone."

The Lost Boys exchanged small smiles, looking relieved. Only Kyle noticed how upset I was.

"You're going on an adventure without me?" My voice only wobbled a little bit.

"Of course I am," Peter said in his lofty way. "Girls don't go on adventures. Especially not Wendy girls."

Peter gave me that shrewd judging look. I hadn't seen it since the Never birds chased off the pirates. It was like the past few days had never happened. Like he didn't know me anymore. Like I was just a random Wendy girl, someone he wouldn't have brought to Neverland if Kyle hadn't nagged him. I pressed my lips together tight, determined to keep them from trembling.

Then I clenched both fists and said, "What do you think we've been doing then?"

Peter strolled closer, walking over the empty air carelessly. "You should give me something," he said with his smug, dangerous smile. "You know, like a queen gives her emperor. Like a tribute."

"Uh-oh," Kyle said in a low voice.

Pan was just pulling rank—proving who was in charge—and we all knew it.

The Lost Boys froze, watching us wide-eyed.

Peter pointed at my golden coat. "I want that, Wendy girl."

It was so unfair. What Tiger Lily had said wasn't my fault.

I yanked the coat off and threw it. Peter caught it one-handed. The heavy material hit his palm with a slap.

He shrugged the coat on. It fit perfectly. He looked wonderful, and he knew it.

It made me even madder to see how much he was enjoying himself. When he turned to go, I couldn't stop myself from saying, "What? You don't want the crown, too?"

Peter turned back, and I knew he hadn't thought of it. I knew what he was going to say before he spoke.

"Of course," he said, raising his chin in his new majestic way.

So I went to the trunk, to Kyle's hiding place. My crown glinted in the crevice right behind my sword. I yanked it out so quickly that I scraped some of the bark off the tree.

When I presented it to Peter with a sarcastic flourish, he only pointed to his head with that irritating smile. I placed it on his head, taking care to use as much force as possible, but he didn't even flinch.

"I'll never forgive you, Peter Pan," I whispered, humiliated.

Kyle murmured something, and Dibs hushed him worriedly.

Peter only shrugged. "I don't care. It's not like you're staying. Remember?"

Then he turned and flew away, disappearing into the trees.

26
I Almost Don't Get a Christmas Present

"Don't worry," Dibs said. "He goes off on adventures by himself all the time. It's not personal."

I sent Dibs a hard look. Of course it was personal.

Dibs looked at the ground, shuffling his feet. "He would've done it to any of us," he said softly, and I realized that Dibs had been trying to comfort me.

"Maybe I'll just go *home*," I said, crossing my arms over my chest and imagining Peter's face when he realized I was gone.

"*No*," said Kyle, Button, Prank, and even Dibs, so forcefully that I felt a little better.

"You can't leave before *Christmas*," Kyle added.

I didn't have the heart to tell them that I had to leave before the real Christmas started.

By the time we finished decorating the Christmas tree, it was so dark that Button built a fire just beyond the tree. Prank had produced some blue crystals that looked suspiciously like sapphires. They winked and sparkled in the firelight like real Christmas lights.

While we stood admiring our handiwork, Dibs came out from behind the Tree Home holding something silvery in his hands. They were ribbons.

"Where did you get *those*?" Prank said with a snort.

Dibs placed one on the tree carefully. "I think they were my mother's," he said in a low voice.

Even Prank couldn't tease him after that. "I'll go, uh, get us some dinner from the grove."

"Me, too," Kyle said, and I had the feeling that he was hoping to run into Pounce there. Button followed them wordlessly.

Since no one else was around, I flew over to help Dibs. He was standing on the ground, but I wasn't sure if that was because he had lost his happy thought or because he'd decided the lower branches on the Christmas tree needed more decorations.

"You said your mom left, right?" Dibs said, giving me a long, measuring look that reminded me of Peter. "But she's coming back, isn't she?"

I frowned, not sure where this was going. "Yeah."

Dibs looked down at the ribbons draped over his arm. "You're lucky. I miss mine every day."

I missed mine, too. Suddenly, I wanted very much to be home.

"Do you remember her?" I asked, taking a silver ribbon and flying up to hang it carefully on a branch. "Your mother, I mean."

"A little," Dibs said softly. "Prank has forgotten his mom completely, and Kyle is forgetting his. I think that's why they love Neverland so much."

Sadness filled me slowly, and I started to fall, the happy thought of Christmas draining away. I landed on the ground next to him, and Dibs took a shaky breath. If I missed my mom even though I knew I'd see her again soon, Dibs *had* to miss his so much more. No wonder he was hoping for a temporary replacement.

He rubbed his face with his fists, and when he looked up at me, I couldn't help but notice that the skin under his eyes was wet.

I put my hand on his shoulder. I had thought it many times before, but it was much, *much* harder to say out loud. "I'm sorry I can't be your mother, Dibs."

"It's not easy for us, you know," he said with an embarrassed sort of grin. "As soon as we get used to a Wendy girl, she has to leave again."

I swallowed hard. I had always thought Dibs was just

mad at me. But maybe he refused to like me because he was afraid to miss me when I had to go home.

He turned back to the Christmas tree and lay another ribbon on a branch. "Even Peter is different since you came."

I snorted, disbelieving.

Dibs scowled. "It's *true*. Maybe he's been in Neverland too long, but he didn't even feel like having adventures. The only time he ever perked up was when he was fighting Hook."

I remember how bored Peter had seemed when we first arrived in Neverland, and I knew Dibs was right. I didn't say so, though. It seemed like an awful thing to say out loud.

"I hope Peter doesn't go back to the way he was after you go home," Dibs said with a sigh. "But maybe he can't. You kind of made some big changes around here. Tiger Lily and her tribe really aren't our allies anymore, but, I mean, we're friends with the mermaids. That'll give us some fresh adventures."

I didn't want that to be true. The Grove of Food Trees flashed in my mind—the way the Cubs and the Lost Boys sat side by side. I didn't want to be the person who ruined their friendship forever. "I'm sure that it won't last. You said yourself, Tiger Lily will get over it."

"Don't worry, Wendy girl," Dibs said with a trace of his usual scorn. "*You* won't have to deal with it. *You're* going home. Peter knows that too."

Suddenly, what Peter said before he left made a lot more sense.

I looked away, jaws clenched. I didn't want to forgive Pan just yet.

I had thought of several ways to get back at him.

One was leaving Neverland despite the Lost Boys' protests. Unfortunately, I didn't know how to get back, and the Milky Way isn't really the best place to wander around, lost.

I also considered flying off after Peter and joining his adventure, just to show him he couldn't boss me around, but I didn't want to leave the Lost Boys, especially when Kyle was still a little shaken up.

Or we could start Christmas without him.

"Hey, Dibs—I planted a new food tree over there this morning," I said, pointing. "Would you mind checking to see if it grew? Please? You can have first pick."

Instead of arguing with me like I thought he might, Dibs just sighed deeply and went.

When he disappeared behind the leaves, I waited, knowing what he would find.

"Candy canes! Gingerbread men! Chocolate!" Dibs cried, and he was so delighted that he crowed, exactly like Peter.

I grinned, glad *someone* was cheered up.

By the time the other Lost Boys got back, Dibs and I had stripped all the Christmas treats from the new food tree. I let the Lost Boys eat the sweets and cookies instead of the chicken tenders they'd gathered at the grove.

Peter still hadn't come back.

Watching Button devour his fourth gingerbread man in a row, I announced, "It's time to open presents."

"Really?" Kyle and Prank said together. Kyle had chocolate around his mouth.

"I thought Christmas was supposed to be tomorrow," Button said doubtfully.

"That makes this Christmas Eve," I said. "Plenty of families open presents on Christmas Eve."

"But there aren't any presents under the tree yet," Prank said, looking under it with a suspicious expression. "Doesn't Santa come at night?"

"I have some presents," I said, flying up the Tree Home to retrieve my backpack. Button had helped me finish Peter's present too, but I was actually leaning toward *not* giving it to Peter and keeping it instead. Under the circumstances, I didn't feel too bad about that. "Okay, everyone—close your eyes."

They did, and I flew around, passing out leaf-wrapped packages.

"Maybe we should wait. Peter was really looking

forward to this game," Dibs said cautiously, but when I pushed a gift toward him, his hands closed around it.

Personally, I thought that if Peter was going to go on adventures by himself, then it was definitely all right to play all the best games *without him*.

I clasped my hands in my lap, trying to contain my excitement. "Okay, you can open your eyes now."

The leaves I had used to wrap the presents were on the ground in less than a second. Button examined his present, pulling out colored markers and examining them in the light of the fire.

"It's an art kit," I told him. I leaned forward and whispered, "So that the next time you draw stuff for your staircase, it won't wash away in the rain."

Button looked up at me. He didn't say anything, but he practically glowed with happiness.

"I got a book," said Dibs, sounding disappointed.

"It's about Peter," I said, pointing to the title on the spine. I figured that Dibs would want it the most. "I can read it to you later, if you want."

Dibs pretended not to hear, turning to Prank. "What did you get?"

"These weird colored loops," Prank said, squinting at them in the dark. "They're floppy."

"They're rubber bands," I explained. I took one from him, held out my thumb and index finger like a gun, and attached the rubber band to them. I took aim at the Christmas tree and then bent my thumb, sending the band off into the branches. "See?"

Smirking, Prank retrieved the rubber band that I had used to demonstrate, and he stuck it in his pocket like it was something precious. "I think I'll be able to find a use for it."

"Don't aim at any mermaids," I told him sternly, and he deflated slightly.

"Look! Look what I got!" Kyle shouted, holding his present up high.

I smiled. I was particularly proud of Kyle's present. I had found it on the playground at school a few weeks ago, and I had never taken it out of my backpack, not even when I packed for Neverland.

"What is it?" Button asked.

"It's a car," Kyle said triumphantly.

"What's a car?" Prank asked.

"You drive it places," said Kyle. "Sometimes you can get up to a million miles per hour."

"Not *that* fast," I said, half smiling.

"It's too little to do all that," Prank said doubtfully.

"Maybe it gets bigger," Dibs said.

"Big enough so that you can get inside?" said Prank.

"No," I said, hunching my shoulders forward. This wasn't going the way I'd planned. They weren't exactly showing the proper Christmas spirit. "It's just a toy."

"A toy," repeated Dibs, Prank, and Button dreamily.

I hadn't realized how popular a real toy would be in Neverland. Kyle used both hands to cover his present protectively.

"Let me have it," Dibs said, making a grab for it.

"No, it's mine." Kyle drew back and curled over his new toy.

Prank loomed over Kyle too. "Come on. I'll trade you."

"Cut it out, Lost Boys," I snapped. "To give is better than to receive."

That stopped the fight. They stared at me.

"*Why?*" asked Dibs in a way that made me suspect that he had never heard anything that sounded so silly.

"I don't know," I said, suddenly uncomfortable. "My parents and teachers say it."

The Lost Boys exchanged looks, starting to grin. "Look who's turned into a mother on us," said Prank, and I didn't say anything, not sure how to argue. It *did* sound like something Mom would say.

"She's not really a mother," Button said thoughtfully. "More like a big sister."

"Like Peter's kind of like our brother?" Prank said.

"I always wanted a sister," Kyle said.

Dibs, Prank, and Button agreed.

I felt myself starting to Pretend even before I decided to do it. I was Ashley, Wendy girl as no Wendy girl had been before, big sister to all Lost Boys, their protector and playmate.

My toes and fingers tingled, but besides that, I didn't really feel any different.

Maybe—well, maybe I had *already* been acting like their sister.

"Nobody's given Ashley anything," Kyle pointed out quietly.

All the Lost Boys exchanged guilty looks, and I realized that none of them had thought of it.

"It's okay," I said, smiling sheepishly. I meant it. "Being your sister's a pretty good present."

"Peter put something under the tree this morning," Dibs said slowly.

"I bet it's for Ashley," Button said.

"I'll get it!" Prank dashed forward.

Kyle raced him and won, placing the present in my lap as proudly as he would've been if he had picked it out himself. It was wrapped in a piece of blue cloth, and I unwound it slowly, already beginning to feel very sorry for starting Christmas without Peter.

"It's a belt," I said, fingering the leaf pattern etched into the brown leather.

"Why would Peter get Ashley a belt?" Dibs asked. "I thought girls were supposed to like jewelry."

"Or clothes," Prank said, counting on his fingers. "Or flowers, or chocolate."

"I bet it's for her sword," Button said. "The rest of us have one."

I looked at the belt again, and all my anger disappeared.

I felt sad and happy at once.

Neverland's Christmas just didn't feel complete without Peter. The Tree Home felt a little quieter—a little emptier—without Pan to boss us around.

I wanted him to come back.

"Thank you for the present, Ashley," Kyle said, throwing his arms around my neck and hugging me tightly.

"Yeah—thanks, Ashley," said Prank, and Button echoed him.

Even Dibs thanked me, with his new book open in his lap. Apparently, he liked his gift much better after he saw the illustrations.

All the Lost Boys stayed up late with their new presents. Dibs went to bed first. He had eaten so many treats that he gave himself a stomachache and had to go lie down. Prank perfected his aim on his rubber band gun. Button drew tiny, precise pictures on some crumpled paper I had found at the bottom of my backpack. Kyle fell asleep among the roots of the Tree Home, still making car engine sounds in his dreams, and Button helped me carry him up to his hammock bed.

Then I settled myself a little above the Lost Boys, waiting up for Peter on the branch where his house sat, my new sword belt in my hand. I wanted to apologize for having Christmas without him. I wanted to give him the present I made for him.

"Don't worry, Ashley," Prank said, pulling his blanket all the way up to his chin. "Peter's fine. Sometimes, he doesn't return for *days*."

That wasn't very comforting.

I leaned my head against Peter's house and prepared myself for a long night.

I must have fallen asleep. One minute, I was staring into the dark, determined to stay awake until Peter returned. The next, I woke, still clutching my new belt.

A terrified bell-like wail filled the air, and a flickering light zipped frantically over the Lost Boys' hammocks.

"What's wrong, Tink?" Dibs said, sitting up.

"I thought that she was banished," Kyle said, rubbing his eyes sleepily.

"She says, it's Peter," Button whispered. I couldn't see his face in the dark, but he sounded horrified. "He's been captured."

27
Tink Asks for Help

For a moment, everyone held their breath.

"Impossible," said Dibs fiercely.

"That's not funny, Tink," Prank said. I had never heard him sound angry before.

"Do you honestly expect us to believe that Buttercup was captured yesterday, Kyle was captured today, and Peter is captured now?" Dibs said. "That's a lot— even for Neverland."

But I believed her right away. The idea of Peter Pan captured was too scary to joke about.

"She says it's her fault," Button said softly.

That made everyone quiet again. It was probably the

first time Tink ever admitted something was her fault.

"What *happened*?" I asked.

The fluttering light froze and turned slowly to face me, saying something in a low, frustrated chime.

"She says that they were trying to get rid of you, Ashley," said Button.

That didn't surprise me.

I mean, the other kidnappings had been my fault. If I hadn't stolen Hook's hat, would the pirates have captured Buttercup? If I hadn't gone to fight the pirates, would the Cubs have laid the trap that got Kyle?

My new friends were better off before I arrived. I waited for someone to say so, but no one did. Not even Dibs.

That didn't stop me from feeling guilty.

The fairy started chittering so quickly that Button struggled to translate fast enough. "Tink watched us rescue Kyle. She knew how much Tiger Lily hated you—her words, not mine," Button added quickly, but I shook my head, not caring. "Tink had a plan. She knew how easy it would be to convince Tiger Lily to help."

"You needed someone big enough to make it happen," I said to Tink in a cold voice.

The fluttering light bent a little. Tink hung her head.

"Tink says she made the nets for the traps. She started as soon as she was banished and she finished yesterday morning," Button translated. "After we rescued Kyle, Tiger Lily strung them up, somewhere close to our tree, where they knew Ashley would have to fly. They were going to give Ashley to the pirates."

"That's not very smart, Tink," Kyle said. "You know that Peter would have rescued her."

We didn't have time to talk about how intelligent her plan was. "Tink, do the pirates have Peter?" I asked impatiently.

Tink's chimes started to sound like wailing again.

"Tink says she and Tiger Lily waited in the tree to trap you. Finally, a figure zoomed by. They saw the golden coat that the mermaids had given the Wendy girl," Button said, shooting me an anxious look. I forced myself to keep breathing. "Tiger Lily loosed an arrow and cut the rope. The net fell and knocked the figure to the ground."

We gathered close around Tink. I could see how mussed her hair was, how torn her clothes were, and how her tiny hands were shaking as she chimed her way through the tale.

"Tink says that she thought she had won. But she didn't catch Ashley," said Button. "She caught Peter, and he wasn't moving. He wouldn't wake up even when Tink shook him and pulled his hair and shouted."

"Do you think he hit his head when the net knocked him down?" Dibs asked.

"Was he breathing?" I asked Tink. Kyle made little sobs like hiccups in the back of his throat, and I took his hand.

The fairy didn't answer me.

"Tink says she shouldn't have shouted," Button went on. "The pirates, they heard her, and they came. They found the crown that had fallen from Peter's head, and then they found Peter. The pirate with one eye aimed his sword at Peter's throat."

"No," said Prank, pained.

My chest felt tight, like I had to breathe around a knot between my lungs.

Tink was crying so hard that she kept interrupting her story with little bell-like hiccups.

"Smee was with them. He made them stop," Button translated, and all the Lost Boys let out a relieved sigh. I shook my head slowly, still worried. "Smee told the others how delighted Hook would be when they brought him Pan."

The Lost Boys glanced at each other nervously.

"When they started taking Peter away, Tiger Lily attacked them," Button said when Tink went on, "but the pirates captured her, too. Smee called it getting two for one."

I couldn't care less about Tiger Lily.

"Peter," Kyle said in a choked voice. "Captured by pirates!"

"It's the worst thing that has ever happened in Neverland," said Prank with clenched fists.

"What will we do?" Dibs said, starting to panic. "What will we do?"

I began to pace across the air beside Button's bed, thinking hard. Turning the Cubs against the Lost Boys was bad.

But nothing compared to this.

If the pirates killed Peter, this place would never be the same. What kind of Neverland would there be without Peter Pan?

"Please, Ashley." I turned to look at Button, but then I realized that he was still translating for Tinker Bell. The fairy raised her tiny arms toward me. "Please, Ashley, Tink says. There isn't anyone else. Only you can find a way to save Peter."

The Lost Boys rushed into the air, crowding me. I could see the hope in their eyes, and a tiny part of me started to panic too. We only had time for one rescue attempt before the pirates hurt Pan. It couldn't fail.

"Give me a second, everyone," I said, beginning to pace the air again. "I need to think."

I had to save Peter.

The Pirates See Two Peters

*I*t was the best plan ever. If I do say so myself.

This is how it began.

Peter woke and found every pirate in Neverland surrounding him. Some laughed. A few leered. Their captain smiled and smoothed his black mustache with his hook. Peter looked around slowly, testing the ropes that held him and scowling.

I know this, because Prank and I hid only thirty feet from him, hovering on the far side of the ship. We pressed up against the slimy wood and peeked over the *Jolly Roger*'s railing as the mended red sails flapped in the wind.

Black Patch Pat had my golden coat. Since it was too small for him, he had stuffed it into his pocket, like a handkerchief, and I vowed to steal it back.

"Peter, how good of you to join us!" said the pirate captain, smiling. "We've been dying to have you visit for *ages*. Just. Like. This," he added slowly, letting his hook caress the ropes that tied Peter to the deck.

The pirates laughed. Peter raised his chin, eyes glittering in the early-morning light.

Prank curled his fists, furious that they would treat Peter like that, but he didn't move—he was practiced at being sneaky.

"We thought you might want to take a walk," Hook told Peter.

"We've prepared the plank for your enjoyment," Smee added with a smile full of gray teeth. "And Cap'n thought we might make sure you had an anchor on you too. Just so you wouldn't be bothered by flying."

"We've thought of everything, you see," Hook told Peter. "The only question that remains is whether you would like to die *before* your little princess friend, or *after?*"

Peter's gaze traveled to the left, to the right, and finally behind him. There Tiger Lily lay, bound with *almost* as many ropes as Pan himself. She looked at him, gulping.

Then Tiger Lily raised her chin and said, "The Sixth

Amendment in the Bill of Rights clearly states, 'In all criminal prosecutions, the accused shall enjoy—'"

I had to stifle a gasp. That was *my* line.

The pirates looked uncertain, but not their captain.

"My dear princess," he interrupted, "the Bill of Rights is a legal document signed in the United States of America. *You* are in Neverland. We have no laws here."

The pirates laughed smugly.

Tiger Lily glared, but Hook turned to his other prisoner.

"Peter," he sang in his lofty tone. "We *do* require an answer. You *don't* want us to decide for you."

Peter didn't speak, but I could tell he was worried.

Then someone crowed, way high up in the air. All the pirates froze except for their captain. Hook looked up, very slowly, the glee draining from his face.

A figure in green swooped among the sails, his fists on his hips. He wore Hook's hat, and the feather danced as he spun in midair and rocketed up past the mast.

Peter stared, stunned.

"What do you think you've captured, you stupid old man?" the figure in green shouted, and he crowed again.

"*Now,*" I whispered to Prank.

Prank nodded once, with a determined sort of smirk. Then he crawled over the ship's railing, across the deck, toward the cannons. Not one pirate turned away from the two Peters. I flew in the opposite direction, around the rail of the *Jolly Roger*.

"Did Peter have a twin?" asked one of the pirates. "Have there always been two of them?"

"No, of course there haven't been two of them," Hook said with a snarl. "Pan? Is that you?"

"Who did you *think* it was, you codfish?" shouted the figure zipping through the air.

I heard a bell-like trill and then a bunch of pirates grunting as they hit the ship's deck, face-first. I had told Tink to distract everyone while I freed Peter. She was taking her job very seriously. She had stolen a small dagger from Black Patch Pat, and, hugging the hilt with both arms, she wielded it as well as Peter wielded his sword.

"Can't be Pan. We've already got him here," Smee said, kicking Peter in the ribs, but he started to sound a little doubtful.

"Remember these?" shouted the figure wearing Hook's hat as Polaroids began to flutter down to the deck.

Smee picked one up. "Cap'n! Cap'n, look! It's just like I said—Pan, he's developed some new sort of magic."

I peeked over the side of the ship, right next to where Peter was tied.

Her dagger in her arms, Tink sent Noodler sprawling over the deck with a swift kick to his backside.

Prank knelt unnoticed, hidden behind a cannon, sawing at one of the ropes.

Hook bent scowling over the Polaroid that Smee held out to him. "But it looks just like Pan—a tiny, little Pan."

"Aye, Cap'n."

"Just like *that* one, and *that* one," Hook said, stabbing a finger first toward Peter on the deck and then the figure weaving dizzyingly among the sails.

"It's as we feared, Cap'n," Smee said, looking very serious behind his spectacles. "Pan has made a copy of himself."

"Is that true, Pan?" Hook shouted up to the flying figure. "Have you made a copy of yourself?"

The flying figure crowed again and said, "The great Pan is never caught!"

Peter's mouth opened. Furious now, he was a second away from shouting and ruining everything. I leaped soundlessly over the deck and clapped a hand over his mouth. When he tried to twist his way free, I whispered, "Just think how you'll trick them, Peter."

He stopped struggling, and he looked over his shoulder at me, blinking in astonishment. I let him go.

Two pirates turned toward us, but Tink rushed at them with her dagger.

"Pan, if it *is* you, come down and fight me, you insolent boy," Hook shouted.

Peter watched the figure wearing Hook's hat cartwheel around the crow's nest.

"That's Dibs," I told Peter, using my sword to saw at the rope. He had several layers of it around his shoulders, and elaborate knots tying down each hand separately. "Wow, the pirates certainly weren't taking any chances on letting you work yourself free."

"Of course not," Peter said in a low voice with all his usual cockiness.

Rolling my eyes, I smiled. At least Peter's ego hadn't been injured during the capture. I sliced through the ropes around his right hand, freeing it.

"If you don't come down," Hook shouted to the figure in the sky, "then we will *shoot* you down. Ready the cannons!"

"I knew you would come, Ashley," Peter said in a completely different tone. Almost like he was grateful.

I paused. A Wendy girl had never rescued Peter before, but then again, before I came to Neverland, Peter never *needed* rescuing.

I shouldn't have stopped sawing at the ropes. Just at that second, one pirate ducked past Tink's guard and noticed me helping Pan.

"Hey, it's the Wendy girl!" Smee yelled, pointing at me. "Cap'n, it's a rescue!"

I looked across the ship. Prank gave me a thumbs-up and drew his two swords to deal with the small crowd of pirates who had come to ready the cannons.

Turning back to the ocean, I shouted, as loud as I could, "Now!"

Black Patch Pat and three other pirates started toward Peter and me, weapons raised.

I drew my sword, stepped in front of Peter, and rose a few inches off the deck. "You might want to hold on," I told Peter.

Grinning, Peter grabbed the ship's rail with his free hand. Tiger Lily's eyes widened.

The *Jolly Roger* began to tilt.

From the look of things, it was even harder to walk than when I had dropped the anchor.

"Not again!" cried Black Patch Pat, falling forward a few feet from us. The three pirates behind him tripped over his head. Black Patch Pat howled in pain when one of them fell on his hand.

I snatched my coat back with a triumphant smile.

Captain Hook grabbed Smee, who grabbed a rope beside him to keep them from falling over.

A couple of the pirates near Prank toppled over the side. The cannons rolled into the sea right after them. Prank twirled both his swords and danced along the ship's railing, pleased with himself and his rope-cutting skills.

I saluted him with my blade and shrugged my coat back on.

"Watch out!" Prank shouted, pointing to my right.

I ducked out of the way just before a shining hook sliced through the air, exactly where my head had been. The pirate captain had snuck up on me, clawing his way along the ship's railing to reach us.

"What have you done to my beautiful ship?" Hook shouted.

"Just enlisted a little help," I said, pointing over the railing toward the water.

The mermaids lined the starboard side, pushing against the wood and swimming with all their might. Their tails threw up great big splashes, sparkling in the sunlight. Seeing Hook, Buttercup bared her teeth fiercely and gurgled breathless orders to her comrades.

Button, who I'd sent to fetch our allies, left the mermaids and flew up onto the deck, just in time to engage Smee, who had been about to attack my other side.

Hook swung at me again, this time with his sword.

20 The Crocodile Gets Another Nibble

I barely blocked with my own blade in time.

I know that back in my bedroom, I'd said I wanted to cross swords with Hook. But right then, Hook was at the bottom of the list of pirates I wanted to fight. Especially since I hadn't had a spare moment to Pretend I was a great swordswoman.

"Hook is mine!" Peter cried indignantly.

"Well, you're all tied up at the moment!" I replied sharply. "And I'm not just going to let him slice me up."

Hearing how scared I was, Hook smiled and thrust his blade at me. I knocked it out of the way frantically. I didn't have enough experience with swords, and

Peter was really the only one good enough to match him. It was much easier to make plans and be tricky.

"Then get me my sword, and I'll cut *myself* free," Peter said, exasperated.

"Where is it?" I asked, glancing around the deck.

"You don't mean this little trifle, do you, my dear?" asked the pirate captain.

Hook carried Peter's golden sword in his own belt. He tapped it lightly with his hook, and a small metallic chime rang out.

"Uh-oh," I said.

I looked around for help. Prank had already lost one of his weapons, but he battled Noodler fearlessly anyway. Button dodged his way past three pirates. Sensing that the trick was over, Dibs had come down to the deck and was dashing back and forth with one hand on Hook's hat, making half a dozen pirates chase after him. Tink was in trouble—Black Patch Pat had her pinned to the mast, and she struggled to get free as the pirate brought his dagger closer and closer.

We were still outnumbered.

Luckily, one of us had not yet made an appearance.

"Kyle!" I shouted.

Above the cliff just a few hundred yards from the *Jolly Roger*, the littlest Lost Boy flew out of the trees. He smiled and pointed his sword at the pirate ship with a wordless yell.

A dozen of Tiger Lily's Cubs burst through the leaves, echoing Kyle's war cry.

"What the—," Hook started to say, watching the braves grow ever closer.

We hadn't had enough time to get the whole tribe fairy dust, so we created an alternate way of flying. The braves sailed over the water, each holding on to two Never birds.

Seeing them, Peter crowed with delight.

From the water below, Buttercup looked up at me. "Now?"

I nodded. She gave an order, and every mermaid stopped pushing at once.

The *Jolly Roger* wobbled back into place. All the pirates who had been getting to their feet were thrown off balance again—including the pirate captain.

I shoved him hard, just for good measure, and as Hook began to fall backward, I snatched the golden sword from his belt and tossed it behind me.

Peter caught it and crowed again, this time with pride.

He sliced himself free in an instant.

By the time the captain scrambled to his feet, Peter was already there.

"Miss me, Hook?" he asked. Then, with a sword flourish, he attacked the pirate so fiercely that you would've never guessed that he'd spent the last few hours all tied up.

Only Tiger Lily remained. She was bound too tightly to move, but she watched me with pleading in her dark eyes. I knew what she wanted.

"You know, I really did want to be your friend," I told her, scowling. "But you lost a lot of points when you threw Kyle to Croc, and now that you've hurt Peter, you *really* aren't one of my favorite people."

Tiger Lily lowered her gaze, ashamed.

But I sliced her ropes anyway. For Pounce's sake, not his sister's.

The Cubs landed with soft thumps all around us, and the deck got a lot more crowded. The pirates gulped nervously, seeing themselves surrounded. All it took was one bloodcurdling shout from Pounce, and the pirates started running, panicked, in all directions.

Spot landed on my shoulder briefly and rubbed her head against my hair. Her feathers had turned as blue as the sky.

"Thanks!" I told the Never bird, and she flew off with the rest of her flock.

Hook passed behind me, deflecting all of Peter's attacks with a nervous sort of scowl. Sensing victory, Peter crowed again.

Then I heard the sound that I had been waiting to hear.

"Bells on bob tails ring, making spirits bright," sang

a voice that came from the water.

Peter turned to me with one of his proud grins. "You *have* been busy."

"What?" Hook asked. "What is that singing?"

I shrugged demurely, peeking over the side of the ship again. Humming together, the mermaids jabbed at the huge reptile with tridents, herding him even closer.

The crocodile surfaced and splashed, and we heard snatches of "Jingle Bells."

"It's funny," Peter said to the pirate captain. "Usually you start screaming when Croc gets this close. Seeing as he took your hand. And your ear."

Captain Hook stiffened. He turned slowly to look into the water, horrified.

"I don't think he knows that the crocodile has changed his tune," I said.

Prank appeared on my other side, snorting as Kyle, Button, and Dibs joined us.

"Jingle bells, jingle bells, jingle all the way."

"Lost Boys—and Ashley," Peter added hastily when I gave him a look. "On the count of three."

"One," said Kyle, raising his sword.

"Oh, what fun it is to ride—"

"Two," said Dibs with an expectant sort of smile.

"—in a one-horse open—"

"Three!" I shouted, and we all stabbed our blades

toward Hook at once.

"—sleigh!"

The only way he could dodge was backward, and he fell right over the side, into the water, where the crocodile was waiting.

"Whoops," Prank said with one of his wicked grins.

"Think he'll really be eaten this time?" Kyle asked Peter as we watched the scene below. The pirate captain tried to swim away frantically, but the mermaids turned him back around with their sharp weapons.

"Jingle bells, jingle . . ."

The crocodile swam forward, opening his jaws wide, but Hook raised his sword, screaming shrilly.

We weren't the only ones looking. The pirates lined the starboard side, their hands raised high, the Cubs' knives at their backs. Smee stood closest to us, holding a white flag of surrender and watching his captain wrestle with the crocodile.

"Jingle all the way . . ."

"Would you look at that?" Smee said softly.

"Smee, you stupid dog. What are you doing, Smee?" Hook cried, sputtering out seawater. "Save me! Save me, Smee!"

"Oh, what fun . . ."

Smee began stroking his chin. "It occurs to me now, Cap'n, that I've been wantin' a promotion."

"Yeah," added Black Patch Pat. "I've been meaning

to talk to you about the way you treat us. Sometimes, you ain't nice—ain't nice at all."

Tiger Lily gave a cry. One by one, all the braves ran across the deck and dived into the sea on the port side, swimming for shore. Pounce smiled and waved before he went, and Tiger Lily held my gaze for a long minute.

"And the food!" cried a pirate in an apron, who was probably Cook. "It's terrible!"

Finally, the princess nodded deeply with a very small smile. I figured that was her version of *thank you*. Then she dived off too and was gone.

"*Smee!*" Hook screamed.

As we turned our backs to him and flew toward shore, the sound of splashing was the only thing we heard.

Then, thrilled with their victory, the Lost Boys began to crow. I turned to Peter with a grin, expecting him to join them.

But Peter looked grim as he sheathed his sword. "We better get you home," he told me, and my smile faded.

30
I Don't Miss Christmas

*D*ibs was the only Lost Boy who didn't look shocked.

"Take her home?" Button repeated.

"But why?" said Prank.

"She just saved your life!" Kyle said angrily, as if he thought Peter was trying to punish me.

I said nothing, watching Peter. It didn't *seem* like he was still mad at me, but I guess he was eager to get rid of me before I caused any more trouble. After all, I *had* gotten him captured.

"It's almost Christmas," Peter said flatly. "It's time for her to go back."

I swallowed hard. I wanted to do *both*—to stay in Neverland *and* go home for Christmas.

Kyle dropped abruptly, and Button and I barely caught him before he hit the water and got all his fairy dust wet.

"Sorry," he said hoarsely when he could fly on his own again. "I just lost track of my happy thought for a sec."

That made me drop a little altitude too.

"Time to say good-bye," said Peter. He didn't look at me.

Buttercup appeared in the water below us. She had overheard, and she had already started crying. Her tears were green. "You *have* to come back to visit. Promise you will."

I flew down and clasped her hands, but I didn't promise. I didn't know if I could. "Thank you for everything, Buttercup."

"You'll always be a friend to the mermaids," she said. She kissed my cheek swiftly and swam away. I don't think she liked good-byes.

"You *will* come back, won't you?" Button said. "To be our sister?"

I looked at Peter, who still wouldn't look me in the face. I shrugged, spreading my hands helplessly. I couldn't come back without someone to bring me fairy dust and lead the way.

"If you wanted to be a Lost Girl," Dibs said softly, "I would be okay with that."

"Yeah, you're almost as good at playing tricks as I am," Prank said brightly.

"Thanks," I said, blinking my eyes a lot and hoping nobody would notice.

Kyle couldn't contain himself any longer. He launched himself at me, and I opened my arms.

"You're my favorite Wendy girl," he said, hugging me tightly.

"I thought I was your *first* Wendy girl," I said, smiling in a trembly way. "I'm the only one you know."

"No matter how many Wendy girls I meet, you'll still be my favorite," Kyle said, as fiercely as he'd ever protested being little.

"Do any of you want to come?" I said, my voice cracking just a bit. "Some of the Lost Boys did, you know. With the original Wendy."

Kyle's face brightened. He considered it. I know he did, but Peter gave the Lost Boys such a sharp look that they hastily said, "No."

I guess they didn't want to leave Peter all alone either.

"Wait for me at the tree," Peter said firmly, like he thought that the Lost Boys might still change their minds. "I'll be back soon. Tink, go get Ashley's backpack and catch up."

The little fairy chittered agreement and zipped off

to the island ahead of everyone else.

The Lost Boys waved and said good-bye once more, sailing toward shore on a gust of wind.

Kyle waited around as long as he could, holding my hand, until Peter took off in the opposite direction, saying, "Let's go."

"'Bye, Kyle," I whispered, squeezing his hand, and then I flew off after Peter. My chest hurt, like suddenly my heart had swelled too big to fit behind my ribs.

I had thought that it would stop hurting as soon as I left Neverland and its magic faded from me. I'd thought that being the Lost Boys' big sister was just Pretend. But as we passed out of Neverland and into the starry sky, my toes and fingers stopped tingling, and my chest *still* felt too tight to breathe well. By the time a small, familiar light appeared and passed me my backpack, my eyes had filled with tears. Shrugging on the straps, I blinked them away without a sound. I really *would* miss the Lost Boys.

Peter flew ahead of me, leading the way. I couldn't see his face, but he must've looked fierce. The stars parted ahead of him, scurrying out of his path. He never looked back, never once checked to see how I was doing.

He only spoke to me one time—about halfway there. "What did you wish?"

Since he hadn't turned, it took me a second to realize that he'd been talking to me and not Tink. "What?"

"During the thunderstorm," he said impatiently. "What wish did you make?"

I didn't know how to answer. Wishing not to get in trouble seemed so selfish now, especially since I'd caused Peter so much trouble.

Finally, I said, "If I tell you, it won't come true."

Peter was silent until Tink chittered questioningly. "I thought that you wished you would never grow up. That you would stay with us," he said.

Pan didn't say anything more—not the whole flight home.

Instead, Tink kept flying back and forth between us. When she came to me, she chimed encouragingly and patted my cheek with her tiny hand. I smiled a bit, without humor. This was a weird turn of events— Tink comforting me and Peter ignoring me.

But at least someone was still speaking to me. That was the happy thought that kept me flying.

All too soon, we fell through the clouds. Below us glittered the lights of my town, and as we flew lower, I recognized my elementary school and the streets that led home. Everything sparkled in the moonlight. It had snowed while we were gone. Our shadows showed up starkly against the white.

Flying down my street, Tink warmly greeted the

McKinleys' tree, which twinkled with Christmas lights, and she was very embarrassed when she realized there weren't any fairies in it. Then there was my yard and my house, which looked small and unfamiliar and very dark. It didn't look like anyone was home.

I flew up to the second story. My window was still open. The white curtain fluttered in and out, tangling my legs when I landed.

Peter didn't come in at first. He hovered outside, elbows on the windowsill.

Now that I was home, in my own bedroom, saying another good-bye made me feel like crying even more. The house seemed lonelier than ever. I had gotten used to having other kids around.

"Tink, go back and wait for me," Peter said, pointing up at the clouds.

Tink chimed a pert little question, but Peter scowled darkly, his eyes narrowed.

Then she flew toward me, way too quickly for me to dodge. I braced myself for a scratch or a hair pulling, but the only thing I felt was a warm little pressure on my hand. The fairy's arms squeezed my palm, and she lay her head on my thumb lovingly.

Tink was *hugging* me.

Her bell-like voice rang out again.

"She says, 'Thank you,'" Peter said.

I *had* won her over after all. It just took longer than I'd expected.

"Oh!" I blinked really hard again, but it didn't help. My cheeks were wet. Tink let me go, zipping out the window and toward the clouds. "Good-bye!" I called. "Good-bye!"

Apparently, my shouting woke someone up. The house wasn't as empty as I had guessed.

Footsteps thumped in the hall. My bedroom door swung open, and the lights snapped on.

Peter and I flinched against the sudden brightness. Arms closed around me, picking me up.

"Hi, Mom," I whispered, hugging her back.

"Oh, Ashley. Let me look at you," she said, drawing back and searching my face. Her hair was going everywhere, like she'd been running her hands through it all night. She only does that when she's really worried.

"That's—" My dad stood in the doorway, staring past my mother and me. "He's—I mean, the note said, and your mother said, but I didn't believe—"

"It's all right, Richard," Mom said, straightening up a little. "Hello, Peter."

Peter sat lounging at the window, half in and half out of the house. "Hello, Wendy girl."

But he wasn't talking to me. He was looking straight at Mom.

For a second, I wondered why he would call my

mother "Wendy girl," and then I realized what it meant. Grandma Delaney never met Peter Pan. I was related to Wendy Darling on *Mom's* side.

"You went to Neverland too," I said to my mother wonderingly. "*You're* the Wendy girl who made the food trees."

Mom nodded. "A long time ago."

"She wouldn't let me call the police," Dad said.

"That doesn't mean that I wasn't worried sick," Mom said sharply. "Not when it took Peter so long to bring you back. Not with all the pirates and the crocodiles and mermaids who could drown you—"

"I made friends with the mermaids, actually. And I didn't get kidnapped once." (I figured that this wasn't the best moment to mention that the crocodile had eaten her iPod.)

Mom crossed her arms over her chest and raised both eyebrows the way she does when she doesn't believe me. "I *know* how long the trip from Neverland takes. When I talked to Peter, he promised to bring you back today. Then you didn't come back this morning, and I knew that something had gone terribly wrong, and you were in terrible danger—"

"Peter got captured, not me—" I started to explain, but then I worked out the rest of what she said. "Wait, you talked to Peter? You knew?"

With a slow, wide smile, Mom pulled something out

of her pocket. The wooden whistle, the one that usually hung from the frame of her mirror. She raised it to her lips and blew. It didn't make a sound at first, but then the noise came—a hollow sound, like you get when you blow over the top of an empty bottle. But it wasn't coming from Mom.

It was coming from Peter. Sitting on the windowsill, he reached into his leafy shirt and drew out his pipes. They kept whistling very faintly even after Mom stopped blowing.

Dad's mouth hung open a little.

"I had the fairies spell the pipes and make the whistles," Peter said. "So the Wendy girls could reach me wherever I am."

"I knew you were going to be bored when it turned out your dad and I would have to work all weekend," Mom added with a grin. "So I called Peter and asked him to take you to Neverland for a few days."

"She did warn me that you weren't going to be like the other Wendy girls," Peter said with a trace of his usual cocky smile. "I didn't believe her at the time."

I was stunned. Why hadn't I suspected it all along? It seemed so obvious now.

"I told you that you might find a friend," Mom said, her eyes glittering, and I realized that my mom could be *just* as tricky as I was.

I started to grin, but then Mom said sternly, "You're

still in *huge* trouble. Going to Neverland is just fine, but neither of us said that you could take the iPod or the camera with you."

I gulped. I hadn't seen this coming either.

"Well?" Mom asked. "Where are they?"

"Croc has swallowed the iPod," Peter announced.

I gave him a dirty look for ratting me out, but he just seemed a little smug. I could tell he was happy that *he* didn't have parents.

I thought quickly, unzipping my backpack and passing the camera to Dad. "The Sixth Amendment clearly states—"

This time, it was Mom who laughed, not Dad.

"First off, it's Christmas," I began.

"Christmas Eve," Mom corrected. "And we have *yet* to get a Christmas tree."

"I can't deny that I took the iPod and the camera without permission. But really, the camera is perfectly fine," I continued. "I took very good care of it, and I would've taken very good care of the iPod if it hadn't been swallowed by a giant crocodile."

"Well . . . ," Mom said, considering.

I pressed on. "Plus, I brought back presents for both of you."

She was cracking. I sensed it. One more comment would make or break the bargain.

With a self-sacrificing sigh, I added, "Instead of

grounding me, you could take one of my Christmas presents."

"Great idea," Mom said with a sly smile that reminded me of Tink. "You *were* going to get an iPod for Christmas . . ." My mouth fell open. An iPod of my very own! . . . "but I'll just keep it to replace the one you lost."

I started to protest and then stopped, realizing.

The wish that I had made, *this* was how the falling star granted it. The problem was that *now*, I wasn't completely sure that I would *mind* getting grounded if I *also* got an iPod.

"So, she's not in trouble?" my dad said, shocked.

"It'll be different if she ever takes something off-limits without permission again," Mom said, giving me a stern look.

Before we got too carried away, Peter cleared his throat. "I must say good-bye." His gaze slid to my parents. "In private."

Dad got a look on his face like he was going to tell Peter just how rude he was, but Mom only smoothed the hair away from my eyes with both hands. "I'll tell you what. I'll take your dad downstairs and fix us some hot chocolate. When you're done, you come down too. I want to hear all about your adventures. And," she added, smiling, "we still have to see about getting us a Christmas tree."

I nodded slowly. She went to the door.

"Are you *sure* we shouldn't punish her?" I heard Dad ask as he followed Mom to the stairs, and then they were gone.

For a moment, Peter and I only looked at each other.

Then, suddenly, Peter reached out and touched my new sword belt with one finger. "Merry Christmas, Ashley."

"Oh!" I slung off my backpack and dug past Mom's and Dad's presents for Peter's. "I almost forgot to give you this."

Peter took it and turned it over and over in his hands. He began to unwrap it, much more slowly than the Lost Boys had unwrapped theirs.

I tried to think of something to say, something other than good-bye. "Am I your favorite Wendy girl?"

"No."

He sounded so sure that I felt stupid for even asking.

"You're my favorite Ashley," he said quietly, with a very small smile.

The wrappings fell to the floor, and Peter stared at the framed picture in his hands.

"It's us. All of us. At the mermaids' dinner." I couldn't keep myself from babbling. "Button helped me make the frame."

When Peter looked up, I saw his eyes glittered a little, and I knew I wasn't the only one who was sad.

"It's to remember me by," I said softly, but my voice cracked. I knew exactly where he would put it, and I couldn't bear to think that I would be just another memory in his bookcase.

"Why?" Peter said, straightening up with a fierce glare. "Aren't you coming back?"

"*Can* I come back?" I said, beginning to smile.

"I suppose you don't want to *now*," Peter said, folding his arms over the frame and scowling so hard that I knew his feelings were hurt.

"I thought you didn't *want* me to come!" I said happily, throwing my arms around him.

His shoulders stiffened, and I let him go, embarrassed. Then Peter smiled so widely that I was tempted to hug him again.

"I mean, I got three people kidnapped," I pointed out.

"You specialize in rescue," Peter said, and my smile grew. Then he ruined it by adding, "I must've rubbed off on you."

I shook my head fondly. So I wasn't ready when Peter tossed me something. I just barely caught it in time, but then I opened my hand to find another wooden whistle, almost identical to my mother's but a little longer and more slender. I looked up in surprise.

"Use that to call me when you need to." Peter ducked through the window, hovering just outside, with a fist on each hip. "You're pretty good at having adventures, you know."

He waved once and flew faster, the frame tucked under his arm, joining a little zigzagging light. Clutching the whistle, I watched as he and Tink disappeared through the clouds, and then I watched a little longer.

I was sorry to see him go. After everything that had happened in Neverland, it was hard to believe that I could have any adventures in normal life.

But I was wrong. After all, it was Christmas Eve.

"Ashley!" my mom called up the stairs as the front door creaked open. "Hurry! I called the Christmas tree place—we only have half an hour before they close."

"Your mom is making them hold a pretty one for us," Dad added.

I tore my gaze away from the sky. "Coming!" I shouted, sprinting for the stairs.

Acknowledgments

I have *so* many people to thank that I hardly know where to start! Many readers don't realize how many individuals work on a book before it hits the shelves, but I feel lucky to have met several of the following in person.

First off, I want to thank the lovely team who supported this novel when it was just an idea. Barbara Lalicki, my wonderful editor, who wanted to hear Wendy's story and asked me to tell it. Maria Gomez, who read an early version of the first chapters and laughed in all the right places. Laura Arnold, who always had a sympathetic ear when I got overwhelmed. Rosemary Brosnan, who said some kind words that gave me a lot of confidence. And Jena Rascoe, who knew I could do it before I did.

Countless other people at HarperCollins Children's Books have worked hard behind the scenes. Alexandra Bracken, former editorial assistant and copywriting queen, who suggested many brilliant solutions to our revision troubles. Maggie Herold, who is probably the kindest production editor I know. Kathryn Hinds, my fantastic copy editor, who did a really wonderful job of entering Neverland and untangling some fuzzy time lines (among other things). And Erin Fitzsimmons, who made this book look pretty—both inside and out.

Last but definitely not least, I need to add a special thank-you to my family and friends—especially Mom and Dad, who should get the Most Supportive Parents in the World Award. I don't know where I would be without them. And Angela, my dear ex-roomie, who endured me taking over our big yellow couch and talking her ear off about mermaids and Never birds while I worked out the plot of this book.

Thank you all so much!